DATE DUE

C-99	an	OKB	
O-99			
D-99			

W9-DDR-076

DEMCO

V

SPARKS FLY

SPARKS FLY

•

Cheryl Cooke Harrington

AVALON BOOKS
THOMAS BOUREGY AND COMPANY, INC.
401 LAFAYETTE STREET
NEW YORK, NEW YORK 10003

PRINTED IN THE UNITED STATES OF AMERICA
ON ACID-FREE PAPER
BY HADDON CRAFTSMEN, BLOOMSBURG, PENNSYLVANIA

Mom and Dad, this one's for you.
With special thanks to
Sheila Seabrook, Moreen Miller, and the Ladies of the Train,
to
Jesse and Glenn for the gift of wings,
and to
V., who generously shared his love of flight.

Chapter One

"Hello? Anybody?" Logan shrugged the heavy backpack off her shoulders. It hit the dock with a thud, shattering the early morning silence, echoing around the lake like distant thunder in the still morning air. If that didn't get Mitchell Walker's attention, nothing would.

She stretched, rolling her shoulders to ease the stiffness of thirty-three hours on a northbound Greyhound. Indigo Bay, Ontario, was the end of the line—a ragtag collection of buildings perched on the side of the highway like birds on a wire. A rusty red sign over the window of the general store promised *Ice Cold Coca-Cola*, but the store, like everything else in Indigo Bay, was closed at 5:30 on a Tuesday morning.

The place was exactly the way she remembered it, though, from Riggs' Texaco where the bus had dropped her, to the squat and sturdy-looking redbrick post office at the crossroads, right on down to the Gray Goose Laundromat and Bales' Marine at the lakeshore. Even the old Aurora Hotel hadn't changed, still promising *Moosehead –eer on Tap* in flickering blue neon. It had been ages since she'd thought of that missing "B." Did the locals still say "gimme an ear" when they bellied up to the bar? She smiled. What else? More than just good to be back . . . it suddenly felt as if she'd never been away.

Somewhere in the distance a dog barked, a door slammed— first sounds of morning in Indigo Bay. But still no sign of Mitchell Walker. She glanced at her watch, pulled a rumpled sheet of paper from her pocket, and read the brief message once more, two lines in her own haphazard scrawl. *Meet at the public dock in Indigo Bay. Tuesday morning, 5:30 sharp.* She'd underlined the word ''sharp'' after the Ontario Northbound flight agent had warned her, twice, to be on time. Logan heaved an exasperated sigh. Hopefully, Mr. Walker was better at flying than he was at keeping appointments.

She felt her impatience ease perceptibly as she gazed across the water to the lush, green forest beyond. So what if he was late? What difference would five minutes make? Or ten? She was here to relax, to unwind, to leave the rat race behind, make a fresh start in a new life. Even so, when a lonely-sounding loon called out to her from across the lake, she was sorely tempted to answer, eager to make first contact with a voice from home. Any voice. Instead, she hoisted the backpack and began to walk.

A floatplane bobbed lazily in the shallow water at the far end of the dock—a deHavilland Beaver if she wasn't mistaken, and a real gem compared to some of the rattletraps she'd flown in over the years. A surprisingly whimsical name, painted in bold red letters on its bright yellow door, brought another smile to her lips. *AirWalker.* With a name like that, it had to be Mitchell Walker's plane. Was it possible she'd found herself a bush pilot with a poetic soul?

That intriguing thought was cut short before she could take another step. Someone was watching, she could feel it. Sunlight flared off the windshield of the Beaver and she raised her hand, shading her eyes against the glare. The interior seemed dark and empty, what she could see of it, anyway. No explanation there for the telltale tingle between her shoulder blades.

She turned, expecting to find her missing pilot waving at her from shore, but the rocky beach was still deserted, and so was the road beyond. The tingle turned into a shiver.

''This is silly,'' she muttered, feeling suddenly foolish. Alone at last and totally spooked by the very thing she'd come so far to find—a little solitude.

Back in Toronto, she'd never felt really alone, although many times she'd longed for that luxury. Even at night, in her tiny third-floor apartment, the rhythm of the city, its people and traffic, were a constant, inescapable hum. Now, after ten long years of background noise, the powerful sound of silence was more than a little unnerving. She took a deep, steadying breath of piney-sweet air and felt herself unwind another notch. The peace and quiet of sunrise on Indigo Bay was a gift, a welcome home, a forgotten treasure—one it seemed she'd have plenty of time to enjoy this morning, thanks to a certain tardy pilot.

A half dozen of her customary long, quick strides would take her to the end of the dock, but instead she moved at a leisurely pace, stopping to admire the glint of sun on the water, an osprey soaring gracefully overhead, the trim, efficient lines of the floatplane, the man in the cockpit. . . .

Whoa! From now on she'd pay closer attention to those tingly feelings. The man was slouched in the pilot's seat, arms folded, chin tucked onto his chest. Possibly asleep, but somehow it felt more likely that his oversized dark glasses were just a convenient way to hide from unwanted company. She cleared her throat with a loud ''Ahem,'' but he didn't move a muscle. ''Excuse me . . . hello? Are you Mitchell Walker?''

Silence. Almost as if . . . Good grief! Was he even breathing? Maybe she should climb up there and make sure. . . .

With a grunt, the man turned slowly to face her. Hooking one finger over the bridge of the sunglasses, he pulled them down to the end of his nose and stared at her over the rim. ''Who wants to know?'' The glasses shot back into place with a flick of his finger.

Who wants to know? she thought. He wasn't dead, just incredibly rude.

Logan's backpack hit the dock again as she planted both

hands on her hips. "*I* want to know," she snapped, using her sharpest teacher voice, the one guaranteed to grab the attention of the tough guys in her ninth-grade science class. Of course, the sleepy stranger with his stubbled chin and sour expression had next to nothing in common with her bark-but-no-bite young students, a fact that hit home when a pair of broad, black eyebrows arched above the frames of his dark glasses. One of these days she was going to learn to think before she spoke.

"Guilty as charged," muttered the man, pushing open the door and climbing out onto the dock.

Well, what d'you know? Apparently some teacher tactics worked as well on grumpy bush pilots as they did on teenaged boys. She watched as he folded the sunglasses and dropped them into his pocket, grumbling something about a city girl lost in the woods and how his day was rapidly going from bad to worse.

City girl? He couldn't possibly be talking about her . . . could he?

Heaving a deep sigh, as if resigned to something he'd really rather not do, he turned and slowly raised his head. In the split second after his gaze collided with hers, Mitchell Walker stopped grumbling. The frown slowly faded, replaced by a wobbly sort of half-smile. Not such a sourpuss after all, thought Logan, tossing out her hastily formed opinion.

He was tall, broad-shouldered, a lot younger than she'd expected, with a tousle of raven hair straggling across his forehead and curling softly over his collar. His jeans and faded denim shirt looked relaxed, comfortable, tried and true. And so did the man who wore them.

He swiped at the tangle of hair to push it away from his face, grinning sheepishly as it tumbled back into place. Shrugging, he offered a brief handshake, although the gesture would barely qualify as such, so lightly did his fingertips brush her palm.

"Mitch Walker. And you are . . . ?"

"I'm your passenger, Mr. Walker." Logan bit down on her lip, stopping herself just short of laughing out loud. Obviously, she was not what he'd expected. Maybe she should give him a break, confess the truth, let him know who she really was right up front. It would make their trip together a whole lot easier. But not half as much fun. "So, when do we leave?"

"You?" He shook his head, retreating into the shade beneath the broad yellow wing of the Beaver. "Uh-huh. I'm sorry, Miss, but you . . . you're . . ."

I'm what? she wondered, biting a little harder. The answer was painfully obvious. Mitchell Walker had already written her off. Just another city girl. Talk about hastily formed opinions!

"What I mean is, there must've been a mistake. My passenger is some old guy from Toronto. He's headed north to Casey Lodge. Planning a long stay, too, from the look of all the stuff he wants to cart along."

"Some old guy?" She thought of her namesake and swallowed another laugh. Walt Logan was "some old guy," all right. A local legend. To hear Gramps tell it, Walt used to fly that old Twin Otter of his blindfolded, with both hands tied behind his back. Once, stranded on a remote lake during a violent summer storm, Walt helped bring a baby girl into the world. Her grateful parents thought it only fitting she be named in Walt's honor. Gramps was awfully fond of reminding her that it could've been worse. She could've been stuck with "Wally." Better than "some old guy." "Let me guess. Is the old guy named Paris?"

"Yeah. Logan Paris. Why? Do you know him?"

"Know him?" Logan's grin finally got the best of her. "Mr. Walker, I *am* him."

Mitch fished the sunglasses out of his pocket and planted them on his nose again. For a moment, she thought he might join her out in the sun. Instead he moved farther into the shadow cast by the wing, resting his elbows on the strut and crossing his legs at the ankles. He studied her skeptically. *"You're* Logan Paris?"

Definitely not what he'd expected. She nodded, uncomfortably aware of the intensity of his gaze, unsettling despite the dark glasses. For one long moment he said absolutely nothing.

Logan tugged self-consciously on the brim of her cap, brushed a bit of lint off her blue University of Toronto sweatshirt, tucked the scrap of paper back into the pocket of her jeans, and just for good measure, examined the toes of her new work boots. Nothing missing, nothing undone. So what on earth was the man staring at? And why did that stare make her feel so thoroughly uncomfortable?

He frowned. "Well, Logan Paris, you're late."

"Late? Now just a darned minute. I—" His suddenly grim expression froze the words on her tongue.

He shrugged and made a helpless little gesture with his hands. "And your flight plans have been changed. Because of the fires. You understand." His tone suggested he didn't expect her to understand at all.

Following his gaze westward to a dark and ominous smudge on the horizon, Logan felt her heart stammer and miss a beat as the vision flashed in her mind. Smoke and flame and an endless, lonely night . . .

No! She wouldn't go through that again. Not here, not with Mitch Walker watching. Had he noticed her shocked reaction, the sudden quickening of her breath? She'd probably gone dead pale at the sight of that smoke.

Grabbing the straps of the backpack, she twisted them tightly around her fist, forcing her thoughts back to the present, struggling to calm the pounding of her heart, to ease the painful knot in the pit of her stomach. The fire was too far west to be a threat to Casey Lodge, too remote to be a threat to much of anything except trees. "Looks pretty bad," she said softly, hating the tremble in her voice.

"Getting to be. And they're running short of supplies out on the line."

"They're fighting it?" Things had changed more than she thought. In the old days they'd have let the fire burn.

"Well, yeah," said Mitch, as if her question had taken him by surprise. "They are now. You all right?"

She could feel him watching, wondering, and deliberately squared her shoulders, forcing herself to look up at him, to ignore the sharp whiff of smoke on the new breeze. Fire or not, she wasn't about to fall apart like . . . like some city girl. "I'm fine. Why?" Her voice sounded too husky, but at least it was steady again. Almost.

Mitch shrugged, glancing down at her hands. "You trying to strangle that thing, or . . . ?"

Letting the well-twisted straps of the backpack fall from her fingers, Logan changed the subject as smoothly and as swiftly as she shifted her gaze away from his face. The smudge on the horizon had mushroomed. "What's out there?"

"Ever hear of D'Or-On?"

"Door on?" What did doors have to do with forest fires?

"Pretty hot news around here these days. Mineral exploration. Gold fever."

Ah . . . *d'or.* Gold. So much for his French accent. "It's a mining company, right?"

"Huh! Moving company is more like it—moving in and taking over. One of their exploration camps is out that way. Lots of people *and* lots of expensive equipment." Mitch frowned. "Anyway, they must have some kind of clout, because the Fire Boss is calling up everything with wings, including this Old Beauty."

He spoke quietly, running both hands along the wing strut in a slow, familiar gesture, as if the Old Beauty lived and breathed for him. A touch so tender and loving, Logan couldn't help but imagine how it might feel.

"I can still get you to the lodge today," he said, abruptly turning his attention back to her. "That is, as long as you don't mind making a stop at the line camp first. But—"

"But what?" She felt a blush creep up her cheeks. Mitch was looking at her as if he knew exactly what she'd been thinking. Was he looking at her or the airplane? *Don't think it!* If only he'd take those darned sunglasses off.

She waited, half-holding her breath, staring at his big, strong hands. *Big, strong hands?* Why was she letting this happen? What was it about Mitch Walker that had her so off balance? And wasn't he ever going to finish his sentence?

"Thing is," he said at last, "I've got three drums of fuel in the back. No room for those crates of yours. But I'll make another run, maybe later in the week."

"Oh. Uh . . ." She watched, momentarily flustered, as he pushed away from the strut and moved toward her, pausing to caress the edge of the wing. Suddenly the prospect of seeing him again held a definite appeal. *Say something!* "Sure. I can manage till then."

Forcing herself to stop staring, she cast a hurried glance back along the dock. If her crates weren't already aboard, where were they?

"Don't worry, they're safe and sound."

As if he'd read her mind. Again.

"I left them at the marina."

A smile flickered briefly across his face as he spoke, vanishing so quickly she almost wondered if she'd imagined it. Had he seen that blush light up her cheeks just a moment ago, noticed the way she'd been staring, heard the nervous little catch in her voice? Suddenly self-conscious, Logan made a grab for the backpack. "Well then, what are we waiting for? Let's get going."

"Hey, not so fast." He caught her hand in his, stopping her

with a firm and confident touch, sending a burst of heat spiraling up her arm. Did he feel it too?

She looked up and met his gaze. Not dark glasses now, but startlingly honest blue eyes. They crinkled slightly at the corners as his smile flickered again. What was he thinking? Had he sensed her nervous tension, maybe assumed she was afraid to fly? Or worse—was he *really* reading her mind?

''How much do you weigh?'' That clear blue gaze raked over her as he spoke, sizing her up from head to foot.

Okay, so it wasn't her mind that interested him. Logan tapped a warning on the dock with the toe of her boot, unconsciously falling into teacher-speak again. *''Excuse me?''*

The elusive smile vanished, replaced by a dubious frown. ''That is . . . what I mean is . . .'' He took a quick step back, releasing her hand and shoving both of his into the pockets of his jeans. ''Sorry. It's just—''

''Load balance.''

He looked surprised. Point for the city girl.

''Uh, right.'' His surprise gave way to something approaching interest. ''You've done this before.''

''Oh, once or twice.''

''So?''

''One-ten,'' she admitted, suddenly glad she'd stuck to her diet and lost the extra pounds she'd been carrying around since last Christmas. Her new, trim figure was worth every one of those skipped desserts and every painful hour spent at the gym.

Apparently Mitch agreed, judging from the sly new smile taking shape on his face. Even so, when he hefted her backpack and the smile turned into a scowl, she took a giant step away from him, just in case he was thinking of trying the same thing with her.

''Well, we can always dump something, I suppose.'' Swinging the door wide, he motioned her aboard. ''You do swim, don't you, Logan?''

Oh, great, he's a comedian now.

Ignoring both his joke and his gallantly outstretched hand, Logan braced herself against the side of the plane. The floating dock dipped sharply as she stepped up to the edge, stirring the calm water, setting the plane in motion.

"Uh . . . you might want to grab onto the strut."

She shook her head. *Concentrate.* Three steps on a sturdy aluminum ladder. *Forget graceful, just stay upright, stay out of the water.* She could feel Mitch watching, waiting for her to slip and prove the city girl theory. No way. She'd done this a hundred times before, a simple series of movements that, once mastered, you didn't forget. Just like riding a bike. Or falling off.

The dock pitched again as she stepped off, and the plane responded, the bottom rung of the ladder rising to meet her foot, buoying her upward and then, just as quickly, falling away.

"Not as easy as it looks, eh?"

"Hmm." The man was a master of understatement.

"You sure you don't want some help?"

"No, thanks." He was also much too close, probably ready to catch her if she fell. Darn him, anyway.

"Whoa!" She lurched through the door, narrowly avoiding a painful bump on the head, diving headfirst into the pilot's seat as the floatplane bobbed again. Her face reddened as she scrambled out of his way and collapsed into the passenger seat. She could hear Mitch behind her, chuckling to himself, probably steady as a rock despite the plane's erratic motion. Turning, she found him already aboard, stowing her backpack in the narrow space between her seat and one of three enormous fuel drums wedged into the cargo bay. Each steel barrel wore a fresh coat of red paint and a single white-stenciled word: FLAMMABLE. Hardly a comforting thought.

She felt her heart begin to pound and her flesh grow clammy. What on earth was she doing? Suddenly all she wanted was to get away from the plane, away from Mitch Walker, and most of all, to *stay* away from that fire. It wasn't too late to back out. Gramps wouldn't miss her. He didn't even know she was coming. She could wait right here in Indigo Bay for . . . For what? Mitch had said the Fire Boss was calling up everything with wings. It might be days before she had another chance to go home.

Mitch gave her a knowing, sideways glance as he folded himself into the pilot's seat. "Nervous?"

"No." *Liar!* That clinched it. No way could she turn tail and run now. She forced a smile, determined not to dwell on the impossible irony of flying fuel to a fire, or what might happen if Mitch Walker's Beaver got a little too close to the flames.

He adjusted his headset and began the preflight check—flaps, water rudders, magnetos. Logan watched his slow, methodical motions with quiet interest. It helped to have something to think about. Something to talk about would be even better, but now was not the time. She wouldn't interrupt what she knew was an intensely personal ritual for him—each flip of switch and twist of dial accomplished with graceful precision, as if set to music only he could hear.

The engine caught and revved, settling into a low, steady growl that rumbled through her, comfortable and familiar. She fastened her seat belt, trying her best to ignore the dark plume of smoke on the horizon as Mitch taxied across the lake. It wasn't going to be easy keeping her mind off that fire. Maybe if she concentrated on the mechanics of takeoff, remembered all those lessons with Walt, back when she could barely reach the pedals with her feet . . .

She scanned the controls, listened to the changing timbre of the engine as it warmed, and eavesdropped on Mitch's UNI-COM call. "Kilo-Mike-X-ray, departing the water at Indigo Bay for Lake Opakopa."

It wasn't working. Her teeth were clenched and her hands

had somehow attached themselves to the armrests when she wasn't looking. *No!* She'd never white-knuckled a takeoff in her life, and wasn't about to start now, fire or no fire. Prying her hands free, she folded them in her lap, forcing herself to take one deep breath and then another. *Relax.*

Mitch was laying on the throttle, picking up speed. Logan focused on the green wall of pine trees that hugged the rocky shoreline of Indigo Bay. The pitch of the engine grew higher and higher as they skimmed across the lake's glassy surface. What the heck was he waiting for? *Liftoff! Liftoff!*

She flashed an anxious glance in his direction as her hands clamped onto the armrests. The man looked perfectly calm. Well, why shouldn't he? Loaded with all that fuel, the plane was heavy. It was bound to take a little more effort to get airborne.

Leaning forward, she watched the tips of the shiny aluminum pontoons lift slowly out of the water, watched all those rocks and trees getting closer and closer. The engine whined, as if in pain. She held her breath, bit down hard on her bottom lip, and closed her eyes, tight. If her second chance at life was about to end in a crash, she didn't want to see it.

Chapter Two

"Hey! You weren't worried, were you?"

Logan's eyes flashed almost visible sparks, singeing his pride with a single, furious glance. "Where the *heck* did you learn to fly?"

Uh-oh. Apparently his passenger was not amused. Mitch felt his grin slip away as she turned back to her window, leaving him to swallow his comeuppance, probably hoping he'd choke on it. Served him right. He had no business hotdogging takeoff the way he had, lifting off at the very last second. Shrugging, he fixed his gaze on the horizon, on the seething plume of black smoke that, for the moment, looked a whole lot friendlier than Logan Paris.

It was so unlike him to take chances, especially with a passenger aboard. Especially *this* passenger. *Now wait just a darned minute . . . where'd that come from?* She was nothing special. Just another squeaky-clean city girl, in for a rude awakening about the facts of life in the north. Mitch chanced a quick, sideways glance, surprised to find himself enjoying the feeling of being with her in the plane. He smothered the thought with a mental wet blanket.

Man, you swore off city girls four years ago. Remember? Not something he was likely to forget. Unfortunately. But there was something . . . different . . . about this particular city girl, and whatever it was had been pushing his buttons from the moment she'd set foot on the dock.

13

For a split second during takeoff he'd been certain she was going to grab the yoke, try to lend a hand, or maybe even take control—not something your typical city girl would attempt. Now though, staring out the window, resting her chin in her hand, she seemed a lot less sure of herself. The flash of temper he'd read on her face just seconds ago had vanished, replaced by a wary, thoughtful expression that dulled the fire in her eyes, made her look lost and utterly vulnerable. Made him want to reach out and comfort her.

He risked another, longer, look. She'd tied her fine auburn hair in a loose ponytail that poked through the back of her Jays World Series cap and fanned across her shoulders, gleaming bright against the midnight blue of her sweatshirt. It wasn't hard to imagine how that hair would feel sifting through his fingers . . . like spun silk. He made a conscious effort to keep both hands on the yoke and stifle the stupid grin that seemed to sprout on his face every time he saw her. But he wasn't ready to look away. Not yet. She was, without a doubt, the best-looking company he'd had in a very long time. She smelled good, too, like fresh spring flowers. Lily of the valley, maybe, or . . .

Get a grip! Spun silk? Reach out and comfort her? Right. And get shot down for his trouble. What was that thing she did with her voice, anyway? Made him feel like a kid, caught with his hand in the cookie jar. Huh. Tough lady one minute, scared little girl the next. She was a mystery, all right, in more ways than one. And trying to figure her out was driving him crazy.

What the heck was she doing up here in the wild north country? It was hard to imagine why a city girl would want to go to Casey Lodge. He knew hunters and fishermen who thought the place was too remote. Lucky for her, he'd be around to keep an eye on things. Not that he was interested. Curious, yes. But *definitely* not interested.

* * *

The man was staring again, trying to hide the fact behind those annoying dark glasses. Logan ignored him, gazing out the window at the forest below. It looked so cool and peaceful, so full of life, dotted here and there with tiny lakes, sparkling like sapphires in the bright morning sun. But not for long. An unwelcome rush of reality snatched her breath away. Just a few short miles to the west, a monster raged—a mindless fury of smoke and flame. It seemed the cruelest sort of homecoming, stolen from her own worst nightmare. And every second, every pounding heartbeat, brought them closer.

Fearful, she glanced back at the cargo of gasoline, then focused on the towering cloud of smoke looming dark and ominous in their path. How many times had she counseled her students to get out there and face their fears? Name it, face it, overcome it. Good advice, but was she really ready to try it herself?

What choice did she have? *I am not afraid. I am not afraid.* Logan ran the words over and over in her mind, a kind of mantra, a way to make herself believe. *I am not afraid. I am not afraid.*

"Hey!" Mitch tapped her gently on the shoulder. "You okay?"

"Fine." She nodded as she turned to face him, instantly certain he wasn't buying the stiff-upper-lip act. Even with his clear blue eyes hidden away behind those dark lenses, there was no mistaking the condescending expression on Mitch Walker's face. He'd expected her to fall apart after that stunt-pilot takeoff, and when she hadn't dissolved into a quivering mess of tears, he'd had to take a second long, hard look at her. And a third.

She tried to imagine how she must have looked to him a moment ago, huddled up against the window, chewing on her bottom lip. A frightened child who'd never been off the ground before.

Arranging what she hoped was a cool smile on her face, she

forced herself to meet his glassy gaze and raised her voice a notch to be certain he'd hear her repeated assurance. "I'm fine."

That smile again! What was so funny *this* time? Even if he didn't believe her, surely the man wasn't heartless enough to laugh at someone else's anxiety. She let the annoyance grow, hoping it might take some of the edge off her fear. It worked. The mantra in her mind sounded stronger now, more confident. She could almost believe. *I am not afraid. I am not afraid.*

"I'm glad," yelled Mitch.

Good grief! Had she said it out loud?

"Glad you're fine," he added, as if sensing her momentary confusion. "I need you to do something."

Perfect. She breathed a sigh of relief. Something to do was exactly what she needed. Something to take her mind off the fire. "What's that?"

"Under your seat. Plastic bag."

She leaned forward, groping blindly under the front of her seat until her fingers brushed something cool and smooth. She grabbed hold and lifted it onto her lap—a Day-Glo orange litter bag, courtesy of Bales' Marine. Bold black letters urged *Pitch in, not overboard! Keep our lake clean.*

"We'll stay low," Mitch continued. "Use less fuel that way. But when we hit that smoke . . ."

"What?" As he turned away to scan the controls, Logan lost track of what he was saying. She pulled open the bag and reached inside. Wet towels? What on earth did he want with wet towels? She glanced up to find him watching again and responded with a questioning arch of one eyebrow.

"Trust me, we're going to need them. Put one over your face when we hit the smoke. I'll get us up and out of it as quick as I can, but there might be a few minutes when, y'know, we won't be able to breathe."

Was he kidding?

"And Logan? Remember to give me one, too, okay?"

No, he wasn't kidding. *We won't be able to breathe.* She'd known that suffocating terror once before, long ago, and had grown up praying she'd never have to know it again. Her stomach turned in on itself. This time the nightmare was all too real.

"We'll be fine," yelled Mitch, giving her arm a gentle pat. "Don't worry."

Smiling weakly, she turned back to the window, resting the brim of her cap on the glass, fighting nausea. Far below, the floatplane's shadow rippled across the landscape, looking small and fragile . . . like one of the folded paper airplanes she and Gramps used to make. *Fire burns paper.* She closed her eyes. Things were definitely not working out as planned.

"Get ready," yelled Mitch, dropping below the trees to buzz the surface of a long, narrow lake. "I think we'll see the fire when we clear the next ridge."

I am not afraid. Logan forced herself to sit up straight and tall, facing forward, watching the water, the trees, the sky . . . the smoke.

I am not afraid. What a whopper of a lie! The biggest fib she'd told herself in ages. But pride kept her chin up, her eyes dry. She had something to prove now, not just to herself, but to Mitch Walker, too. His expression, when he looked at her, had changed from amused to concerned, even worried. And somehow his concern was a lot harder to take than his laughter. Well, he was in for a surprise. She knew this country as well as any man and, fire or no fire, she could take care of herself.

She finished pulling the wet towels out of the bag. They felt cold and smelled a little green, like lake water, a summertime smell that reminded her of Gramps and Casey Lodge. Familiar and comforting. It was good to be going home after all these years. She'd been away much too long, and—

"Yikes!" The towels seemed to leap out of her grasp, landing in a heap on the floor as the plane went rocketing upward. Logan grabbed onto the armrests with both hands and held tight, watching wide-eyed as the floats cleared the trees at the water's edge with only inches to spare. She felt as if her stomach had been left behind at the bottom of the lake. The man was out of his mind! She gulped a deep breath and gave him a piece of hers. ''Are you trying to get us killed?''

Mitch didn't answer. He was staring straight ahead, his face an ashen, lifeless shade of gray. Turning back to the window, Logan saw the awful reason why. Smoke. A towering column of thick, black smoke. It loomed in their path like a wall . . . a wall that seemed to go on forever. The fire had to be a lot bigger than he'd expected.

Panic welled up inside her, intense and demanding. Oh, how she longed to give in to it, let it sweep her away, beg Mitch to turn around now and fly them to safety. Instead, she grabbed for the towels, quickly leaning over to wrap one around his neck, pulling it up to cover his mouth and nose.

Those men on the ground were counting on him, counting on her, to deliver the supplies they'd need to fight the fire. Panic wouldn't help them. Or her. And it certainly wouldn't help Mitch.

Smoke billowed around them, seeping in at every door and window—an acrid, choking cloud, a creeping evil that filled the cockpit and burned her eyes. Gagging, she buried her face in the towel.

Smoke. Even through the layers of wet cloth, it caught at her throat and seared her lungs. Smoke. It filled her senses, clouded her mind. They were still flying . . . climbing . . . the pitch of the engine told her that much. But it was the only thing she knew for sure. What if Mitch passed out, or lost control of the plane? She couldn't see him, couldn't help him, she could only try to trust him. Trust had saved her from a fire once before. But so much had been lost. Forever . . .

* * *

"Logan?"

No air. She couldn't answer.

He yelled again, urgently now, and brushed his hand through her hair. "Logan, are you all right?"

"O-okay." She gasped for breath, swiping the towel across her eyes as the air cleared. It couldn't have taken much more than a minute to climb above the smoke, but that minute had seemed like an eternity. And now Mitch was peering at her through the haze as if he thought she might have expired. For a while there, she'd thought it herself.

"I'm okay. W-what about you?"

"Hey, no problem." He tugged at the towel, pulling it off and dropping it onto the floor between the seats. "Fires are part of the game plan around here. I grew up breathing smoke."

He made it sound so easy, so matter-of-fact. He had no idea.

"Hey!" Gesturing out the window, Mitch seemed about to say more. He never got the chance.

Below them, smoke rolled and churned, a dark, angry ocean. And up through the waves came fiery tongues of orange flame, bright showers of sparks and cinder. Superheated air, rising in violent swells, slammed into the little plane, one bone-jarring impact after another, tossing them across the sky like some flat-bottomed stone skipping wildly across the water.

The air was hot inside, too, and growing hotter by the minute. Beads of sweat had begun to form on Logan's forehead and trickle down her cheeks, but she didn't dare release her grip on the armrests to swipe them away. She watched, transfixed, as Mitch struggled to keep control of the plane. Muscles knotted across the backs of his hands and strained against the soft blue fabric of his shirt. She followed his gaze across the control panel, from attitude indicator, to mag-compass, to altimeter, and back to the horizon, his face a mask of determined concentration, jaw clenched, chin jutting forward. His sunglasses, dangling precariously from the visor, broke free to bounce across the console and onto the floor. And then, as if fired from a slingshot, the plane broke free.

A moment of weightlessness and eerie silence left Logan holding her breath. It took a few seconds to adjust to the quiet, to realize that it wasn't really quiet at all. The roar of fire and wind had overwhelmed even the drone of the Beaver's engine. They'd made it! They were still alive, still flying! Her pent-up breath exploded, half sigh, half laugh as she wiped the damp towel across her face.

''Some ride, huh?''

Mitch flashed a smile as he spoke, but she had the feeling it was forced cheerfulness. He sounded exhausted, and rightfully so. Tugging on his shirt, he tried unsuccessfully to peel it off. It stuck to his sweat-drenched shoulders and back until she helped him pull free.

''Thanks. I was starting to feel like the main course at a barbecue.''

He snagged the towel off the floor and mopped his shoulders and neck while Logan tried her best to avoid staring at what she'd uncovered. Instead she looked out the window, hoping to spot the small lake where they'd make their landing, but drifting smoke made seeing much of anything next to impossible. There was plenty to see in the cockpit, though. Words like taut and tanned sprang instantly to mind, followed closely by an unexpected giggle. Good grief, anyone would think she'd never seen a man before!

Mitch glanced down at his bare chest and then at Logan, breaking into a smile she suspected was more than a little self-conscious.

''You don't mind, I hope?''

She shook her head, fighting another childish giggle. What on earth was wrong with her? Shock? Euphoria? Yes, that had to be it. She was giddy with relief, glad to be alive. Oh, what a glorious chest!

"No, I don't mind. It's just . . ." A snicker bubbled to the surface. *Quick! Think fast—cover your tracks.* "It's just . . . it's still so hot in here. And I'm glad we're okay."

"Not the nice relaxing trip you were bargaining for, huh?"

You just had to make a smart remark, didn't you? "I've made it a policy to always prepare for the worst." Shrugging, Logan fanned herself with the towel.

He laughed. "Well, between having me for a pilot, and this fire, I guess you've put your policy to the test."

Chapter Three

"There! Is that the lake?"

Logan was certain she'd seen the ground just a second ago—green trees, blue water—but the image winked out almost as quickly as it materialized. Nothing more than a ghostly mirage. Or a bit of wishful thinking on her part.

"That's the one," yelled Mitch, banking into a steep turn. "Opakopa. Better hang on."

Hang on? Her fingers had already formed permanent dents in the armrests. Not exactly a notable start in the "proving him wrong" department. She sighed. With any luck he'd be too busy navigating to notice.

"Pretty calm right now," he continued, "but you never know what the winds will do this close to a fire."

Comforting thought. She peered out the window. The air was crystal clear at this altitude, all sunshine and pale blue sky. But below them, dark and deadly, a shroud of smoke lay heavy over the earth. Had Mitch seen the lake, too, or was he still flying blind, relying on the compass and some kind of pilot's sixth sense?

"Don't worry. It's there."

How the heck did he do that? She'd barely had time to form the thought and there he was, ready with an answer. "Where? I don't—"

The sudden sinking feeling that gripped the pit of her stomach and snatched her words away had nothing whatsoever to do with

22

Mitch Walker's strange brand of telepathy. This was seriously scientific—the perfect demonstration for one of her classes on the laws of physics. They were going down!

She scanned the controls, sucking in a deep breath as she locked her gaze on the altimeter. A little more air in her lungs wouldn't help them defy gravity, but it sure couldn't hurt.

"Wait for it," said Mitch.

His voice was calm, steady as a rock. Too bad that rock was falling out of the sky at the moment. She had to remind herself to exhale. Mitch, on the other hand, seemed perfectly confident. Talk about blind faith!

"Should be able to see it . . . right . . . about . . ."

I am not afraid. I am not afraid. Turning back to the window, she watched the dark cloud of smoke growing closer. Not seething now, but thick and eerily stagnant, like a pea soup fog. For one shuddering heartbeat as they sank beneath its surface, she glimpsed her own pale reflection in the window. Wide-eyed terror. Then a welcome flash of green. Trees?

". . . now!"

They dropped into clear air, trailing wispy plumes of smoke behind the wing tips. She heard a crackle from the radio as Mitch flipped the switch.

"Opakopa, it's Kilo-Mike-X-ray, we'll be on the water in two. You guys ready for company?"

He sounded entirely too pleased with himself. Logan heaved a sigh of relief as she pried her fingers out of the newest set of grooves in the armrests. Right at the moment, although it pained her to admit it, she was feeling pretty darned pleased with him, too.

As they left the smoke behind, she leaned forward in her seat to watch the flurry of activity below. There was a small clearing at one end of the lake, and people were running out of the woods, waving up at them.

Mitch guided the plane in a slow, easy circle, then settled

onto the water like a big yellow goose. A perfect landing. Followed by a moment of perfect silence. Strangely unsettling after more than an hour of roaring engine, blazing fire, and gale-force wind.

She let her eyes fall shut, listened to the sound of her own heart beating, the gentle lapping of waves against the floats, and willed herself to relax. Her hands slid away from the armrests; a stretch chased some of the tension from her shoulders. This wasn't so bad. They'd be airborne again in twenty minutes, and then . . . Next stop, Casey Lodge. *Almost home!*

Her eyes flew open. Beyond the window, across a narrow stretch of dark water, one windswept white pine stood guard on a rocky islet. *Home.* Such a beautiful word. A beautiful place. Rugged and wild and—

Mitch interrupted her pleasant train of thought with a loud and colorful curse. "Er . . . sorry." He groaned, shooting an apologetic glance in her direction.

She shrugged. Pretty tame compared to some of the stuff she'd heard in her inner-city school back in Toronto. "What's wrong?"

"No dock." He dropped the headset onto the console and studied the rocky shoreline of Lake Opakopa. Worry lines creased his forehead as his frown deepened. "Wicked rocks. It'll be tricky unloading those barrels."

Logan followed his gaze ashore. Where the water stopped, a solid wall of granite and green began. The clearing she'd seen from the air was little more than a narrow, rocky crescent, strewn with jagged-looking boulders, the only sign of civilization a cluster of grubby canvas tents hugging the forest edge. No place to beach a floatplane. But surely this wasn't the first time he'd unloaded cargo without a dock. Walt used to do it all the time. She'd even helped out once or twice.

"Shouldn't be that big a problem, should it? I mean, I . . . I . . ."

Oh, boy! Two more buttons and his broad, perfectly sculpted and brilliantly suntanned chest would be hidden away again. She sighed, wishing she'd paid more attention to that particular bit of fine northern scenery while she'd had the chance. *Now cut that out!* She swallowed, hard. Hadn't she been about to say something? Oh, right . . . unloading. ''I can help.''

He chuckled, a low intimate sound that brought an instant flame to her cheeks.

''You?''

''I . . . uh . . . What?'' Good grief, she'd been hanging out with teenagers for so long, she was beginning to act like one. What on earth was the matter with her? She tried her best to work up a serious, teacherly expression but, judging from the silly grin Mitch was wearing, she wasn't succeeding.

''You'll help, eh?'' His grin faded. ''I don't think that's such a good idea.'' He reached down, retrieving his sunglasses from the floor, dusting the lenses off on his shirt before settling them on the bridge of his nose. ''Just stay put, okay? The floats on this beauty cost a fortune. I can't afford any accidents.''

Pushing to his feet, Mitch squeezed between the seats and into the cargo bay. Stooped low, with barely enough room to manoeuver, he loosened the restraints that had held the drums in place during their wild ride through the fire, then edged his way to the door. Swinging it wide, he yelled a greeting to the three men waiting on shore.

''Yo! Let's get this done.''

The men splashed into knee-deep water, still wearing their work boots and bright yellow fire suits, carrying long wooden planks and coils of rope.

Mitch hesitated in the doorway, studying her over the back of the pilot's seat. ''These guys know what they're doing, Logan. Just stay out of the way, okay?''

Stay out of the way? ''Right.'' *Wouldn't want the city girl to break a nail.* By some miracle of self-control Logan stayed silent. After all, they were still a long way from Casey Lodge, and he was the only ride around. She could wait a little longer to prove her point. But boy, did he have it coming!

Turning in her seat, she watched as Mitch set the anchors and helped the men build a makeshift ramp with the boards and rope. It took two of them to wrestle the first barrel of fuel to the doorway, and all four to ease it down the ramp and away from the plane. The Beaver bobbed and rolled, strained against the anchors, twisted and turned. Three times the barrel nearly got away from them, setting off volleys of profanity that rivaled the boys' locker room in volume and creativity.

"Hey!" yelled Mitch, over a particularly vivid string of expletives. "Lady on board, remember?"

Unfortunately. He didn't come right out and say it, but watching him struggle with the barrel, she figured the regret was implied. He'd expected a man and got stuck with her instead.

Enough was enough. She might be a "lady," but she was no hothouse flower. And she didn't need Mitch Walker to take care of her, no matter how well-intentioned his efforts. The man obviously had a lot to learn about women.

Pushing aside the thought that teaching him a thing or two might be a whole lot of fun, Logan opened the passenger door, and slipped into the shallow water. She gave a whoop of surprise as it flooded into her boots and soaked the legs of her jeans.

"What the heck are you doing?" yelled Mitch from his post in the cargo bay.

Logan didn't answer. She'd forgotten how cold a northern lake could be, even this late in June. So cold, it took her breath away, left her gasping with surprise.

"Hey! Get out of the water!"

She ignored him, snagging one of the tether lines and wrapping it snugly around her arm. Feet planted wide, she leaned back, using her weight like a third anchor to steady the plane.

"Good job!" yelled one of the men. "Hold tight, little lady. That's just what we need."

Hold tight? Good advice, but not so easy to follow. She felt the heels of her new work boots sinking deep into the sandy bottom of the lake as the icy water inched higher. Just her luck to find a weed bed instead of a nice solid rock to stand on. It was hold tight, or land flat on her back in the water. Not the best way to prove a point.

The plane bucked like a wild horse as Mitch and the men rolled the second barrel out, then the third. Logan held her ground, shoulders aching, muscles burning. Which was worse, the pain in her arms or the fact that she'd lost all feeling in her toes? Good grief, couldn't they move a bit faster?

City girl. No way! She squeezed her eyes shut and tightened her grip on the rope. One way or another, before their day together was over, Mitch Walker was going to start seeing things differently.

"You can let go now."

Mitch wasn't quite sure what to do or say next, a disturbing state of affairs for a man who'd spent a lifetime avoiding awkward situations. Think before you speak. Plan before you act. Good, reliable, *sensible* strategies that had never let him down. Until today. First, that ill-conceived and totally out-of-character takeoff back at Indigo Bay, and now . . . now, his left arm had somehow draped itself around Logan's shoulders before the thought of doing so had even entered his mind. To his utter astonishment it felt right, natural, as if their time together spanned years instead of mere hours.

Don't make any fast moves, said the voice of reason, loud and clear inside his head. *Just put the arm down, back slowly away, and nobody gets hurt.*

Darned if that arm didn't hold her a little closer instead. And darned if he wasn't enjoying the results. She smelled even better up close, and her baggy blue sweatshirt hid a trim and tiny figure, soft and round in all the right places. But strong, too. She wasn't afraid to challenge herself.

He pried the rope from her tightly clenched fingers, felt a shiver course through her, and eased a bit closer, wanting nothing more than to shield her from the cold. Her gentle curves seemed to fit against him, as if she were meant to stand by his side.

Her eyes fluttered open. Green eyes with little flecks of hazel. Clear and shining and—

"Sorry if I *got in the way.*"

Oh-oh. Maybe he should have listened to the voice of reason, after all.

Mitch pulled away, following a cautious two steps behind as they slogged toward shore. What was she so steamed about now? If anyone had a right to be angry it was him, not her. He wasn't in the habit of making his passengers work for their ride, or drenching them in cold lakes, either. Things like that made *AirWalker* look like a third-rate hack instead of the first-class charter service he'd worked so hard to build.

Not that he didn't appreciate the help. Logan had really come through in the crunch, probably saved him a hefty repair bill on the float, too. And what had she gotten for her trouble? Cold, wet, and unappreciated. *Hello . . . earth to Walker?* He felt like such an idiot. No wonder the woman was steamed. Maybe it wasn't too late.

"I, uh . . . I guess I owe you one, Logan. Not a scratch on the Old Beauty, thanks to you. Quick thinking."

She kept walking, striding up onto the beach, kicking stones out of her way. Turning to face him with her hands planted firmly on her hips, she regarded him with a thoroughly indignant expression. *"Quick thinking?"*

Oh, boy. Now what?

"What I was *thinking,* Mr. Walker, was that you ordered me to stay out of the way. And I would have, too, only . . ."

Ordered? Was that what she thought? He'd only intended to spare her from the cold water. That and . . . well, maybe spare himself the worry of looking out for her. And the floats. Now *there* was something better left unsaid! Judging from the look on her face, though, he'd better say something, and fast.

"Only . . . what?"

"Only I couldn't stand to watch you ruin that beautiful old plane. What were you trying to prove?"

"What? I wasn't trying to prove anything. I was just . . ."

"Just what?"

The truth . . . but not the whole truth. "Well, trying to avoid . . . that." He pointed, losing the battle he'd been waging to avoid staring at Logan's legs. Her jeans, dripping water, clung to every perfect curve like a second skin. "You, uh . . . you got wet." *Oh, good one Walker. State the painfully obvious.*

He looked up and found her studying him, amusement dancing in her luminous green eyes. Her laughter sparkled in the air, instantly banishing the tension between them.

"Yeah, well . . ." She pointed at his soggy denims and slowly shook her head. "I'm not the only one."

"True enough." Mitch flopped onto the cobbled beach, feeling more than a little surprised by the sudden rush of pleasure her laughter had triggered. "Listen, next time I tell you to stay out of the way . . . well, you can just tell me where to go. Okay?"

"It's a deal."

Hmm. It was entirely too easy to imagine her taking him up on that. "So . . . where'd you learn your way around floats?"

Logan sank onto the stones beside him, so close her arm brushed softly against his as she unlaced her boots and pulled them off. She never got the chance to answer his question.

"Hey, Walker," boomed a loud voice.

Mitch turned, watching over the top of Logan's head as a familiar figure, a big bear of a man, lumbered out of the woods.

"Boy, am I glad to see you!" shouted the man. "We got a problem."

In that instant, a brisk new breeze swept down from the forest, spreading a smoky haze over the beach. He heard Logan gasp and glanced down in time to see the smile fade from her lips. Grabbing the end of her ponytail, she gave it a nervous twist, then lunged for her boots, dumping lake water onto the rocks before jamming her feet back inside.

Tough lady one minute, scared little kid the next. *City girl, remember? Back off!* Trouble was, he didn't want to back off. He wanted to comfort her, hold her, with both arms this time, and promise he'd keep her safe. Instead, he scrambled to his feet and forced himself to walk away. Things were moving way too fast for comfort in the feelings department and the sooner he put a little space between himself and the city girl, the better.

"How you doing, Andy?"

The big man gave a rueful laugh as Mitch fell into step beside him. "Doin'? Man, I'm *done.* Like toast. And we're short on equipment. You up for a run to Red Lake?"

Mitch looked back at Logan, sitting alone on the beach with her knees drawn up in front of her, arms wrapped tightly around them as if to hold herself together. She didn't need another delay—or another close call with the fire.

"Can it wait? I've got a passenger to deliver."

Andy did a quick about-face. "Pretty lady. Don't you worry, Walker. Me and the boys'll take *good* care of her for you while you're gone."

Mitch shot him a warning glance as they strode back along the rocky beach. "Behave yourself, Twelvetrees. This lady's—"

"Mitch?" Logan scrambled to her feet, tugging on the hem

of her sweatshirt, brushing at the back of her jeans, quick, anxious movements that matched the uneasy expression on her face. "W-what's going on?"

It was the little catch in her voice that did it. Mitch quickened his pace, instinctively reaching out to her as he closed the distance between them, letting his fingers travel the length of her arm before folding her hand in his. She was cold, shivering in the smoke-heavy breeze, struggling to hide her fear and doing a darned good job of it. He knew in a heartbeat that what he'd been about to say to Andy Twelvetrees was undeniably true. *This lady is special.*

"Logan, we're—"

"Well, I'll be gosh darned!" bellowed Andy, elbowing his way between them. "Logan? Logan Paris?"

Before she had a chance to answer, the big man caught her in a bear hug, swinging her off her feet, wrenching her hand out of Mitch's grasp, and planting a sloppy kiss on her cheek.

Was he nuts? Straight off the fire line, his face covered with a crust of black soot, Andy Twelvetrees reeked of smoke and sweat. Definitely nuts.

After a moment of wide-eyed surprise, Logan turned her questioning gaze on Mitch. The best reply he could muster was a slightly bewildered shrug.

"What the heck are you doing here?" asked Andy, setting her gently on solid ground. "Come to fight the fire?" He held her at arm's length, grinning as if he'd found a long-lost friend. "You do remember me, don't you, Shortstuff?"

Shortstuff? This was getting interesting.

Recognition, in the form of a gloriously radiant smile, lit Logan's face. "Andy? Is that really you in there?"

"You bet." The big man swiped his sleeve across his face as if to clean away some of the grime. Of course, since the sleeve was covered with soot, too, it didn't do much good.

"Wow! Andy, you grew!" Her tension of a moment ago

seemed to fade away as she wrapped her arms around him—as far as they'd go, anyway. "Gosh, it's good to see you. How've you been?"

"Uh . . . you two know each other?" *Dumb!* Mitch mentally kicked himself. Twice. Pretty obvious that the two of them knew each other.

"Sure do!" said Andy, beaming like a puppy in love. "Just like her granddaddy, she is. Always ready to pitch in."

Granddaddy? Well, what d'you know? Maybe this wasn't her first visit to Casey Lodge, after all. Had her grandfather made the reservations for both of them? That would explain why he hadn't found Logan's name on the guest list, a more comforting explanation than Casey's worrisome and ever-increasing forgetfulness. But it didn't explain how she knew Andy, or why the big man seemed suddenly unable, or unwilling, to take his eyes off her. A situation Mitch found oddly disturbing.

"So, Shortstuff," said Andy, "Whaddaya say? Wanna spend a little time in the woods with your old pal?"

Think again, big guy. Maybe Logan wasn't just a city girl, but she didn't belong on a fire line. And she was definitely too much woman for Andy Twelvetrees!

Mitch caught her by the arm again, pushing aside the thought that she looked utterly adorable all smudged with soot. "We'd better move. Andy needs me to fly another supply run."

Watching the last blush of color fade from her already pale face, Mitch fought the urge to pull her into his arms. Would she welcome his embrace the way she had Andy's? He sighed. Not likely. But she might welcome an easy way out. "Don't worry, I'll drop you off at the lodge before I go."

Oh, man. Wrong thing to say. Her shoulders had stiffened before the words were out of his mouth. Lesson number one— don't even hint that she might be afraid. What did she think she had to prove? "No big deal. I'll need to refuel, anyway. But, hey, you're welcome to come along for the ride later, if you want.''

''Aw, c'mon,'' said Andy, drawing her attention once more. ''Stay here. We've got a lot of catching up to do.''

Logan's eyebrows arched, a wordless *''You've gotta be kidding,''* then settled into a dubious frown. ''Yeah,'' she said quietly. ''We do. And when you get this fire under control, you know where to find me.''

A look passed between them then, as if something vitally important had been left unsaid. Andy's hopeful grin vanished as she added, ''Take care of yourself, okay?''

He nodded, studying her with a strangely sad expression, dark eyes glittering behind his mask of soot. Without a word he turned back to the smoky forest, while Logan took off down the beach.

Mitch watched her splash into the shallow water and clamber aboard the waiting floatplane, moving as if she'd been doing it all her life. Suddenly *he* felt like the outsider. What did Andy know about her? What shared bit of memory could be powerful enough to wither the big man's smile and send the two of them running for cover?

Does it matter?

Icy water flooded his boots as he trudged back into the lake and Mitch shivered, muttering a curse. It mattered. For some strange reason, everything about Logan Paris seemed to matter to him. Now all he had to do was figure out why.

Chapter Four

"**K**MX to Casey Lodge. Come in?"

Mitch twisted the dial and tried the call again, glad to have something besides the many mysteries of Logan Paris to occupy his mind. Why wasn't Casey answering? They were well within range of that old VHF radio of his by now. *C'mon, buddy, tell me you aren't asleep at the switch. Not today.*

"KMX to Casey Lodge. Over?"

He adjusted his headset, toggling the radio off, then on again, uncomfortably aware that Logan had already clued in to the lack of response from the ground. She was watching him now, chewing on a fingernail and working up a dubious frown. Probably having serious second thoughts about her granddaddy's choice of vacation spot. And who could blame her? First trial by fire, then a dunk in cold water, and now it seemed the innkeeper had forgotten all about her arrival. *Great. Just great.* What else could possibly go wrong?

"Come in, Casey Lodge. This is Kilo-Mike-X-ray, five minutes off the water at Thembi. Anybody home?"

Silence. He shrugged, flashing a brief smile her way. "Casey's probably down at the dock already. No worries, though. *AirWalker*'s about all there is when it comes to air traffic around these parts."

She nodded, turning back to the window without an answering smile, obviously as impatient as he was to see their trip over and done with. Mitch glanced at his watch. Only twenty minutes since the last time he'd checked, but it felt more like an hour. His Old Beauty might be the best darned floatplane in the north, but her cockpit was no place to get to know someone. Conversation meant hollering over the drone of the engine, and neither one of them seemed to have any energy left for that.

He'd spent a fair bit of time watching Logan, though, imagining what he might say when the moment was right—a chance meeting under a starry midnight sky, or a misty morning encounter down by the lake. *What's a city girl like you doing in a place like this?*

Okay. So maybe opening lines weren't exactly his strong suit. But the more he thought about spending time with her, the more impatient he became to make it happen. And that old reliable voice of reason had suddenly fallen silent.

The radio sputtered, a sharp reminder that he'd better get ready to land. One more try. "KMX to Casey Lodge. Over."

Nothing but static. Then, faintly, "Mitch?"

The familiar voice caught him with his finger on the switch.

"Mitch, honey, is that you? Oh, shoot, that's not what I'm supposed to say. Um . . . Kilo, Mikey, Exit . . . Over."

"That's X-ray, darlin', not exit." He choked back a laugh. Ruby Twelvetrees could work miracles in the kitchen, but anything electronic stopped her cold. Right now, she was probably glaring at Casey's old two-way as if the thing had been invented for the sole purpose of irritating her. He couldn't resist teasing, "And *I'm* KMX, remember? *You're* Casey Lodge."

"Watch your step, young man. These gadgets might get the best of me now and again, but I *do* know where I'm at! So . . . where are you?" A brief burst of static filled his headset, then Ruby added, "Over."

"Almost home. Got the coffee ready?"

Silence. Mitch looked up from the controls to find Logan watching. Chin in hand, eyebrows arched, she leaned ever so slightly toward him, looking as if she'd *kill* to know what his contact at the lodge was saying.

Funny he hadn't noticed that sprinkling of freckles on the bridge of her nose before. Or the wisp of auburn hair, trailing across her cheek.

Man, you are in deep trouble.

"It's Ruby," he volunteered, raising his voice so she'd be certain to hear. "Casey's cook."

More than just a cook, Ruby Twelvetrees was Casey's good right hand. But if Logan and Andy were as well acquainted as the two of them had let on, she'd already understand what a fixture the big man's mother had become at the lodge. And knowing Ruby was on the job might ease her mind, not to mention that halfway worried expression she was wearing.

Who're you kidding? You called Ruby "darlin' " and now you're making darned sure Logan knows you weren't talking to your sweetheart.

She nodded, cracking a knowing little smile that left him feeling foolish, like an overgrown, overeager kid. Exactly what she was thinking, most likely.

He brushed at a straggle of hair dangling in front of his eyes, glanced down at his faded blue shirt and threadbare jeans, and decided she was absolutely right. And he looked the part, too. Well, at least *that* was easily remedied. He'd find time for a haircut in Red Lake, shower and shave and make himself presentable. . . .

The radio squawked.

"Casey Lodge? You still there?"

"Over," said Ruby sternly. "You forgot to say 'over.' Over."

He chuckled. "Over and out, Ruby darlin'. I can see the lake. We're home."

*　　*　　*

From the air, Thembi Lake had always reminded Mitch of a crooked finger, a narrow reach of water beckoning him home. And for as long as he could remember, home—a real home—was what he'd wanted more than anything else. The closest he'd ever come to that sense of belonging was right here at the controls of his floatplane. Until Casey O'Malley, that is.

Casey had built his lodge on the sunny north shore of the lake, nestled against the pine forest, its back to a low, sheltering range of knob-topped granite mountains. Guests in the main house had a spectacular view, nearly half a mile of open water, all the way to the ''crook'' in Thembi's finger.

It was the crook that kept them from seeing the lodge now, although he'd caught a brief glimpse of red-shingled roof just a moment ago. Logan had seen it, too, eagerly pointing it out, then leaning forward in her seat to watch their progress over water so glassy it mirrored the lamb's-tail clouds in the late morning sky.

He couldn't have asked for a better first impression. It might even take some of the sting out of the rough-around-the-edges appearance of the lodge. If only she could see the place the way he pictured it—new dock, fresh paint on the boathouse and cabins. No major renovations, but even so, getting it done would take more cash and manpower than he and Casey could scrape together all at once. So, for now at least, it was one small task at a time.

Would Logan stick around long enough to see it finished? He found himself hoping she would, recalling those crates they'd left back at Indigo Bay. No question they were big enough to hold a whole summer's worth of clothing and supplies.

Don't even think it! Mitch tightened his grip on the yoke, tried to concentrate on his approach, but his mind wandered back to Logan. If she stayed a week or two, great. Maybe they'd spend some time together, a pleasant diversion, a summer fling. But any longer . . .

What is it with you and city girls? Seemed like he hadn't learned a single thing in four years. She wouldn't stay. Not once she'd battled the blackflies and come face-to-face with a bear or two. It would happen just like last time. She'd let him start to care, and then she'd run. Back to her safe, boring city, as fast as those gorgeous legs would carry her.

Forget the bears. After their close encounter with the fire this morning, she was probably ready to run already.

The lodge came into view as they rounded the bend, picturesque from this distance, with its weathered red boathouse, rickety dock, and guest cabins strung along the shore like colorful beads on a string. Logan's face lit up at the sight—a smile that packed enough of a wallop to knock Mitch's newly recovered voice of reason for a loop. What could it hurt to spend a little time with her?

Dumb question. And the answer was one he didn't want to consider. Something told him Logan Paris would be worth the risk, though . . . and the pain. He stole another glance, thankful for the dark glasses that kept his interest a secret. Amazing how relaxed she seemed all of a sudden, as if the stress of the morning had fallen away at first sight of the lodge. Too bad he couldn't stay for a while, give her the grand tour himself instead of leaving it up to Casey. But Andy and the trip to Red Lake wouldn't wait. He sighed. With any luck he'd be back in time to join her for dinner. What a treat to see her face across the table, instead of some stubbly-chinned fisherman with nothing but Lakers on his mind. Dinner. This was sounding like a plan.

Assuming you start paying attention! He and Casey always joked about how the Old Beauty could probably find her own way home after so many flights to and from the lodge. But it might be nice to have a conscious pilot at the controls, just for the sake of landing right side up.

He lowered the flaps, laid on the throttle, and greased the little plane onto the water without so much as a bump, cutting power to the engine just in time for a smooth glide up to the dock. Still no sign of Casey.

Docking solo was no big deal, but it meant he'd have to hustle. He shoved open the door and dropped lightly onto the float, hopping from there to the board-and-barrel structure that served as temporary mooring for *AirWalker.* To his surprise, Logan was right behind, giving a joyful little whoop as she bounded out onto the dock.

"Whoa! Hey!" Mitch caught her just in time, slipping his arm around her waist, pulling her close. He made a desperate grab for the wing strut as the dock pitched underfoot. "Think I'd rather stay high and dry this time, Miss Paris, if it's all the same to you."

Logan laughed. "Not afraid of a little cold water, are you, Walker?"

"Careful, now. That sounded like a dare."

"It did?" She steadied herself, hands flat against his chest. Her eyes held a definite challenge. "So, what are you going to do about it?"

He knew what he'd *like* to do about it. Right at the moment, tumbling into the cool, clear water with Logan in his arms sounded just about perfect. The next best thing to a cold shower, and a lot more fun.

"Unfortunately, I've got to fuel up and take off again." He tightened his hold on her, stepping closer to the edge of the dock. "But you don't."

"I . . ." She clutched his shirt, surprise giving way to another burst of laughter. "You wouldn't dare!"

"Oh, no?"

"Lily?"

Logan's head swiveled at the sound of Casey O'Malley's brusque and burly voice, her nervous laughter ending abruptly when the old man appeared at the boathouse door.

"Lily! My stars, it's Lily!"

Lily? Was he hearing things?

She twisted free and hit the dock running, leaving him hanging from the wing strut, mouth gaping in amazement. No way! Logan Paris couldn't possibly be—

"Gramps!"

Lily. Mitch watched her bound off the dock and through the shallows, sprinting across the beach and into Casey's waiting arms. That cold water was looking better by the second. At the very least, he should probably go soak his head. Might smarten him up a bit. How was it possible he'd spent the whole morning with Casey O'Malley's granddaughter and not figured it out?

"Penny for your thoughts."

About all they're worth. Swiping at the trickle of tears on her cheek, Logan drew a deep, steadying breath and tried once again to focus on the scene beyond the dining room window. Mitch Walker and his shiny yellow floatplane were about to take off, heading back into the fire. Just the thought made her wistful and worried. It didn't matter that they'd only known each other for a few hours—seven hours and twenty-three minutes, to be exact. And it didn't matter that Mitch seemed to have more than his fair share of annoying traits—not the least of which was his nothing-short-of-rude reaction to her true identity. Despite his shortcomings, she couldn't help admiring the man. And she couldn't help worrying about his return to the fire zone. But the tears weren't for him.

Brushing another trickle from her cheek, she watched as he taxied away from the dock—if you could call that ramshackle collection of mismatched boards a dock. The tears were for this place . . . her life . . . her home. It had changed far too much in the ten years she'd been gone, and not for the better. Why hadn't Gramps told her? If she'd known he was having hard times, she would have helped, would have come back a whole lot sooner. . . .

Beyond the window, the floatplane took wing, trailing a plume of water that sparkled rainbow-hued in the midday sun. "Go safely," she murmured, masking her concern with a glad-to-be-here smile as she turned to watch her grandfather hobble into the room. She'd tried to convince him to sit, let her run to the kitchen and make them some tea, but he wouldn't hear of it. Casey could be as stubborn as an old bear sometimes, and every bit as grouchy.

"Well, all righty—nickel for your thoughts, then. Is that the goin' rate in the big city? Or maybe it's a quarter, what with that inflation an' all."

Logan's smile suddenly came a lot more easily. She sure had missed his teasing. "A penny will do, Gramps. I was just think-ing about how good it feels to be home. I've missed you *so* much."

The old man's leathery face crinkled agreeably. "Well, Lily-girl, we've missed you, too, and that's the truth."

"Sure enough is," chirped Ruby Twelvetrees as she bustled past him. "Havin' you here'll do your Gramps a world of good, just you wait an' see."

Ruby took the lead, clearing a path for Casey as she crossed the room, shoving chairs and even a table out of his way with a series of well-placed nudges from her ample hips. She depos-ited a tray on the table nearest the window, with two steaming mugs of tea and a plate of biscuits, warm from the oven, topped with dollops of butter and homemade blueberry jam. Smoothing the front of her crisp, white apron, she held out her arms. "Wel-come home, child."

No more tears. Not now. Logan blinked them away as she moved into Ruby's embrace. The woman hadn't changed a bit, from the thick braid of raven hair wound neatly around her head, to the dusky glow of her apple-plump cheeks, to her trademark floral print dress—lilacs today, on a field of pale yellow.

Suddenly Logan's sense of homecoming was complete. Ruby

Twelvetrees had been both mother and trusted friend throughout most of her childhood and, with the possible exception of Casey himself, she knew more about this place than anyone alive. She would know the truth—about the lodge and about Gramps's failing health.

Logan remembered the old man as tall as a tree, hearty and strong, but now he seemed so frail, as if he might fall apart at the slightest breeze. Like everything else around here.

"Oh, Ruby, you haven't changed a bit. But the rest . . ." She dropped her voice to a whisper, letting her words fall with her tears onto Ruby's shoulder. "I shouldn't have stayed away so long."

"Now, now. Don't fret."

Ruby's gentle tone soothed her as it had when she was just a little girl, frightened and crying in the night. *Don't fret.* Code for "don't upset your grandfather."

"Time brings change, child. It's a part of life, don't you know?" She stepped away, holding Logan at arm's length, studying her for a long moment before smiling her approval. "You look wonderful. Too thin, but we'll fix that. Right, old man?"

Flashing a conspiratorial smile at Casey, she shifted the tea and biscuits onto the table and propped the dented aluminum tray against her hip. "Now, you two just enjoy the quiet for a bit. That D'Or-On bunch'll be back from their fishing trip soon and hollerin' for their lunch. Guess I'd better have it ready."

She winked at Logan, adding, "Only good thing about them gold hunters is the business they bring us on their off days."

Turning, she pulled out a chair for Casey. "Come, sit down now and spend some time with your Lily. Just relax and get caught up. I'll bring your footstool in a minute."

"Stop your fussin', woman. Don't want no footstool." Casey thumped the floor with his cane, as if his scowling and growling weren't more than enough to make the point. "I declare, you're 'bout enough to drive a man to drink."

Tucking the cane under his arm, he limped the last few feet to the table unaided, easing himself onto the chair.

Just as stubborn as ever, thought Logan. Maybe he hadn't changed so much, after all. His trademark brush cut, lightened by years of work in the sun, still held more hints of brown and auburn than gray. And his green eyes, so much like her own, seemed bright and alert. He winced once or twice, shifting uncomfortably on the sturdy maple chair, shooting a warning glance at poor Ruby when she made a move to help him. He hadn't always been so abrupt with her. He had to be in a lot of pain, and the fact that Ruby took his back talk in stride could only mean she knew all about it.

"Can't you stay, Ruby? Sit with us for a while?"

"Not this time, child. I've got bread rising. But you come see me later on. We'll have a good ol' visit."

Ruby turned, then hesitated. Worry lines creased her usually smooth brow as she looked back over her shoulder. "The fire ... Mitch says it's pretty bad." More a question than a statement, she waited, obviously in need of a little reassurance. Logan felt her face and hands grow bloodlessly cold as Ruby's words sparked a rush of memories. Who was she to offer comfort? She couldn't even think about the fire without falling apart.

"Oh, my. I'm sorry, child. I shouldn't have." Moving back to Logan's side, Ruby slipped one arm around her, letting the metal tray clatter against the table. "It's just—"

"I know." Touching the older woman's hand with her own, she drew a deep breath and tried to gather her thoughts. "We saw Andy, did Mitch tell you?"

Ruby nodded. Logan imagined she felt her old friend tremble, but that wasn't possible. Ruby was a rock. It had to be her own nerves, rumbling beneath the surface.

"The fire . . ." she began, trusting Ruby to ignore the tentative catch in her voice and hoping Gramps would manage to ignore it, too. "It, um . . . it's big, all right, but it's not on them yet. Just a lot of smoke from the backfires they're burning." She forced a smile. "Andy's fine. Running the show, as usual. But he sure has changed."

Ruby chuckled, banishing the worry lines. "Guess you remember a tall whip of a boy, eh? How old was he? Nineteen? Twenty?"

"Yeah. And I was fourteen and horribly picked on. He was always teasing me about my freckles. And calling me Shortstuff. Boy, I used to hate that." She grinned. "Didn't sound half bad today, though. Made me feel like I'd finally made it home."

"Hmm. Like brother and sister you were. He missed you as much as any of us after your Auntie took you south."

Across the table, Casey grumbled and scowled, folding his arms across his chest. Logan sighed. He wasn't the only one bothered by those particular memories. Even after all these years, mention of the battle between Gramps and Auntie Pearl could still tie her stomach in knots. *Change the subject. Right.* Andy's teasing was much safer ground.

"I missed him, too. Even though he was always grousing about needing his space."

" 'Go away little girl; you're buggin' me again,' " drawled Casey, mimicking Andy's teasing tone. He had the words exactly right, too.

Logan laughed. "I remember. And the only time he didn't complain was when he had me hunting crawlies for his fishing parties. Used to pay me a penny apiece."

"Eh?" Casey straightened. "Only a penny? Hmph. Used to charge me two per."

"Oops," said Ruby, winking slyly in Logan's direction. "Y'know, I'm sure I hear that bread rising. Don't forget, now. Come see me later."

"Count on it." Logan smiled at the older woman's retreating

back and the suddenly vivid memory of warm summer nights in the kitchen, drinking milk with a splash of tea, talking and laughing way past bedtime, and feeling terribly grown-up.

Casey reached for a biscuit, taking a moment to feast his eyes before digging in. ''Mmm. Y'know, for all her fuss an' bother, that woman sure can cook.''

''Mmm-hmm,'' said Logan. She chose a biscuit and lifted it to her mouth, catching a dribble of blueberry jam on her tongue. ''She sure can.'' *And if you think you're going to avoid my questions again, old man, you're sadly mistaken.*

''What happened to your leg, Gramps? When did you start using the cane?''

He paused mid-chew, frowning at her from across the table as if that particular question was the last thing he'd expected to hear.

''Don't be lookin' so worried, little girl. I wouldn't say anything 'happened' to this old leg. Don't always hold me up the way it should, is all.'' He smiled, making her wait while he savored another mouthful. ''Took a little tumble last winter and banged up my hip pretty bad. Lucky thing young Mitch was here to take care of the place, I guess. So then he makes me this walkin' stick and . . .'' He shrugged. ''Been usin' it ever since.''

''He made it?''

''Sure enough. Lots of talent in that young man. Good sense. One heck of a pilot, too.''

She had to agree on that point, but as for the rest . . . ''How much do you know about him, Gramps?''

''Enough, Lily. More'n enough.''

''But, Gramps—''

''Tell me all about that big city of yours. Whatcha been teachin' those youngsters?''

''You're changing the subject.''

''Am I?'' Chuckling, he sipped his tea. ''I dunno, Lily,

there's not a whole lot to tell. Seems like a good match for the both of us. He brings 'em in, I keep 'em happy. Well, me an' Ruby's food, that is.'' He flaked off another piece of biscuit and popped it into his mouth. ''Smart, our Mitch. Lots of good ideas . . . big plans for this old place. Big plans. Take some time, get to know him. You'll see.''

Maybe. Maybe not. She couldn't help remembering the way Mitch had looked at her, his blue eyes full of laughter, warmth, and something else. Something she could only describe as longing. Moments later, once he'd figured out who she really was, his laughter had faded. Suddenly cold and wary, he'd said as little as possible, letting Casey ramble on about how great it was to finally have his two favorite people together, then excusing himself with a promise to join them for dinner. His tone had suggested root canal might be preferable.

She'd watched him walk away, hands clenched, shoulders rigid, looking for all the world like one of her students, caught in a lie and sentenced to a week of detention. But what lies had Mitch Walker told? What did he have to hide?

''What about the D'Or-On people, Gramps? Were they his idea, too?''

''Hmm?'' Across the table, Casey wiped his hands, closing his eyes to savor the taste of Ruby's cooking, with maddening indifference to Logan's question.

''Gramps? *Were* they his idea, part of his 'big plan'?''

He opened his eyes one at a time, chuckling to himself as if she'd said something terribly funny.

''D'Or-On? No, little girl, I'd say D'Or-On was just serendipity.''

Logan gulped a mouthful of tea, trying to swallow her impatience. This was one happy coincidence that seemed a little too good to be true, and she wanted details. ''Serendipity? How so?''

''Well, right about the time young Mitch started flying into

Thembi, those mining company types came around lookin' for a getaway place for their crews. Y'know, somewhere to get them out of the bush for a couple of days. But not *too* far out of the bush, if you know what I mean.'' Casey winked, picked up another biscuit, and considered his first bite.

Logan tried not to fidget, mentally gluing her feet to the floor, sipping her tea with forced calm. She'd begun to feel the time-warp factor the moment she'd stepped off the bus back in Indigo Bay. Life had slowed to a crawl—*less* than a crawl compared to the pace of things in Toronto—and it was going to take some time for her to unwind and get herself slowed down. Hopefully not too much time, because conversations like this one would soon have her at somebody's throat.

''Um, Gramps? You were saying . . . ?''

''I was?'' He grinned across the table at her. ''You need to relax, little girl.''

She laughed. ''Y'know, I was just thinking the same thing. But you *did* stop in the middle of telling me about D'Or-On.''

''Oh, them.'' He gestured dismissively. ''Newcomers. They been stakin' claims, all right. North and west of us. And talkin' about openin' a mine before too long. Pipe dream if you ask me. But they're sendin' us some nice, steady midweek traffic. Add on the fly-in business Mitch is drummin' up, and I tell you, Lily, we might be lookin' at our best summer ever.''

He smiled widely, ignoring her skeptical frown. ''Yep, that D'Or-On money's gonna get us back on our feet. Did you see the new dock?''

New dock? She nearly choked on her tea. He couldn't possibly mean that floating junk heap Mitch had used to tie up the Beaver, could he?

''No,'' said Casey, before she managed to say it aloud, ''don't suppose you did, 'cause it's still in pieces out behind the boathouse. One of Mitch's projects. He's got big plans for the old place, Lily. You won't recognize it by the end of summer.''

That's what I'm afraid of.

Propping her elbows on the table, Logan laced her fingers together under her chin, watching as Casey lingered over his last sips of tea, wishing she felt as sure about Mitch's good intentions as the old man obviously did. He hadn't come right out and said they were partners, but everything he *had* said sure pointed in that direction.

Partners. Where did that leave her? Out in the cold?

No way! Casey Lodge was her home, her past *and* her future. If Mitch Walker had plans for the place, she wanted to know all about them. More important, she wanted to know *exactly* what he expected in return.

Chapter Five

" "Careful, little girl. You might stick that way."

Casey winked, forcing his tanned and deeply lined face into an expression Logan suspected was a pretty close match for her own—brow furrowed, jaw clenched, lips set in a thin, determined frown. He held the pose for a moment, then waggled his wild, bushy eyebrows until she relented with a grin.

"You think too hard, Lily. Always did, even as a babe. Used to tell your mama and papa . . ."

As always, mention of her parents brought Casey to an abrupt and dismal halt. The real surprise was that he'd been the one to bring the subject up this time. It wasn't something he'd ever been willing to discuss.

The light seemed to fade from his eyes as he stared across the table, not *at* her now, but *through* her. His smile vanished and with it went the spark of energy she'd been so relieved to find beneath his frail-looking exterior.

Reaching across the table, Logan gave his hand a comforting squeeze. Maybe now, after all this time, they'd be able to talk about it. She hoped so. There was still so much she couldn't remember about her parents, so much she'd wanted to know when she was growing up and *needed* to know now. But Gramps always said it was better to leave the past alone. It was time to change all that, time to heal the wounds. She held his hand a little tighter.

"I'm not a baby anymore, Gramps. I'm all grown up. And y'known what?"

She paused, half-holding her breath, waiting for a signal from him. Finally, just as she'd begun to fear he wasn't listening at all, he lifted one eyebrow in a spiky question mark. "What's that, little girl?"

"I'd really *like* to hear about my mom and dad. What did you used to tell them?"

He looked doubtful, studied her for a long moment, then shrugged, letting a wistful smile creep across his face. "Told 'em you thought too much and it was their fault for hangin' Walt's name on such a wee 'un. Made you too serious, it did."

Logan laughed. "I remember how I used to wish for a proper 'girl' name. Don't suppose your complaining had anything to do with my wishing, do you?"

"Wouldn't know 'bout that. You always were a smart little thing, though. I recollect takin' you out in the boat one day, and sayin' the water lilies were near as pretty as you. So you decide right then and there that you're gonna have a girl name and it ought to be Water Lily." He chuckled. "Drove your poor mama near crazy for weeks after 'cause you wouldn't answer to nothin' else."

"*Water* Lily? And this was all *my* idea, of course."

"Who else?" He shrugged again. "Real smart little girl you were. Still are. I'd wager our Mitch'll have to be on his toes."

"Oh? You think your new partner *needs* someone to keep him on his toes?"

"Do I—" Casey coughed hoarsely, not quite disguising a laugh. "Stars above, Lily, there you go again. Thinkin' too hard."

"But, Gramps—"

"Nope." Slipping free of her grasp, he tapped a gnarled finger on the tabletop. "I'd say it's my turn to be askin' a few questions. Like why didn't you tell us you were comin'? And how long can you stay? Don't be sayin' a week or two, now. I'm thinkin' all summer, am I right? When'll they be wantin' you back at that school of yours? And—''

''Whoa! One at a time! Boy, you sure can fire off the questions.'' *Too bad you're not as quick with the answers.* But the old man had let one vital piece of information slip. He hadn't bothered to deny that Mitch was his partner. *Now what?*

Logan pulled her hands off the tabletop and folded them in her lap. Judging by the way her heart had begun to pound, it wouldn't be long before they'd be trembling. Why was she so nervous all of a sudden? She'd made her decision, the *right* decision, weeks ago. And no upstart pilot was going to make her back down.

Good grief! Is that what this is all about? She squared her shoulders and gave the swarm of butterflies in her stomach a mental swat. Mitch Walker and his big plans could take a flying leap. This was her life and her decision to make. Well, not hers alone. . . .

''I . . . I'm not going back.''

She waited, holding her breath for real this time, while Casey absorbed the news.

''Not goin' back?''

She couldn't read his tone or his expression. Disbelief, maybe. But what else? Delight? Dismay?

He frowned, knitting wiry eyebrows into one continuous line. ''Why? What's happened? What's wrong?''

Concern. She drew a deep breath, relieved to feel her heart settling into a steady rhythm once more.

''Nothing happened, Gramps. Really. It's just . . . I feel so worn out—worn down. Everything's so hurried in the city. Rush, rush, rush.''

''And . . .''

''No, 'and.' It's just . . . Gramps, I tried, really I did. I know how much it meant to you to see me get an education and have a good career. Now I feel as if I've let you down. I never meant to disappoint you, but I don't belong in Toronto. I've been homesick since the day I left.''

''Disappoint me? Lily, girl, you could never disappoint me. But what about the kids? Your li'l hard cases? You been writin' 'bout them ever since you started teachin'. 'Bout the ones you helped turn 'round. More to it than you're tellin', eh?''

More? Logan let her eyes fall shut for a moment, thinking back over her ten years of exile, six of them living in dormitories, first at the all-girls boarding school Pearl had chosen to ''fix'' her north woods manners, then at the University. Oh, she'd had plenty of friends, but no home, no family. Only an ache in her heart for the people and places she'd left behind. Those kids Gramps was talking about had become the center of her world in the last four years. But life beyond the classroom walls had been little more than a study in loneliness.

''It wasn't easy deciding to leave them. As a matter of fact, it was probably the most difficult decision I've ever had to make. But, Gramps, I was starting to feel as if life was just passing me by.''

She sniffed, swiping impatiently at the tears welling up in her eyes, longing to tell him the rest—that she intended to keep right on turning those kids around, giving them a chance to know life as it should be. But her plans would take some careful preparation and the first step was getting Gramps's blessing for her return. He was studying her, silent and unreadable again.

''Y'know,'' he said at last, in a voice tinged with laughter, ''that's just what your Auntie Pearl said when she twisted my arm 'bout sendin' you down south . . . *'life's just passin' her by up here, Casey O'Malley.'* Huh! Can hear the ol' biddy squawkin' now, just as clear as if she was standin' here. What'd you tell her 'bout this decision of yours?''

''Well, I . . . I haven't exactly told her anything yet. She's in Europe for the summer. I'll write her a letter.''

''Letter, eh? Can't say as I blame you.'' He winked, a totally unexpected reaction. Instead of lecturing her about wasting her education and throwing away her career, he was smiling, thoughtfully stroking his chin, wearing a smug, satisfied expression, as if he'd just caught the biggest fish in the lake.

''All right, little girl, if you're not goin' back to teachin', what're you gonna do?''

She gulped a deep breath. He didn't understand. It hadn't even occurred to him that she'd want to come home to stay. *What did you expect? He's got Mitch and all those big plans. Another mouth to feed is the last thing he needs around here.*

''Oh, my stars!'' exclaimed Casey, as if someone had just turned on all the lights in heaven. ''You're gettin' hitched!''

''No!'' Any other time, she'd have laughed at the suggestion, since her life hadn't exactly been full of candidates for ''hitching.'' But Casey's obvious delight made it all seem considerably less humorous. Was he really that eager to be rid of her for good? She sighed. ''Not even a distant prospect.''

''What? Smart, pretty girl like you? Don't be tellin' me you haven't had lots of suitors.''

''Depends what you mean by 'suitors.' Lots of men who didn't want anything that smacks of commitment. Another thing that moves too fast for me, I'm afraid.''

''Nothin' wrong with being particular in *that* department, little girl.''

''Yeah, well . . . Some people think I'm being *too* particular. Y'know, in the last four years, I've been a bridesmaid five times—don't get me wrong, I was happy to do it, and this isn't one of those 'always a bridesmaid' complaints. It's just that all my friends are married now and starting families. They don't seem a bit worried about bringing a child up in the city. But I think about all the pollution and violence and . . . I'm sorry, Gramps, but that's *not* where I want to make my life. Not where I want to raise a child. And I've been so homesick lately.''

She gripped the edge of the table and met his gaze. It was now or never. *Just say it!* "I . . . I was kind of hoping you'd take me on as your partner, teach me the lodge business. But now . . ."

"Hopin'?" Casey's bushy brows did a dance of surprise across his forehead. "You were hopin? Little girl, you *know* this place is yours, too. Always has been, always will be. Stars above! Just never had it in my head you'd want to come back and run it, is all."

"You . . . you mean . . . Can I stay?"

"Can you stay? You're gosh-darned tootin' right you can stay!"

Casey's expression, a heartwarming mixture of pride and un- bridled delight, put a swift end to her doubts and apprehension. If ever there was a true ear-to-ear grin, the old man was wearing it now. And if his chest puffed up any farther, he'd probably pop the buttons on his red plaid work shirt. *"This place is yours, too."* He'd just made a dream come true. Except for one an- noying little detail.

"Gramps? What about Mitch?"

He looked mildly confused. "Mitch? Well, I dunno, little girl. What about him?"

"He's your partner. Don't you think we'd better ask him how he feels about all this?"

"He'll be tickled pink."

"But, Gramps—"

"You just leave it to me, little girl."

I don't think so. If there was any negotiating to be done with Mitch Walker, she wanted to be a part of it. And if Gramps was serious about taking her on as a partner, this "little girl" stuff had to stop.

"No, Gramps. This is something I think we should do to- gether. If you really want me for a partner, you're going to have to start including me. As grown-up Logan, not Lily the little girl."

"Eh?"

"You heard me." Shoving the sleeves of her blue sweatshirt all the way up to her elbows, as if ready to pitch in and work right away, Logan fired off her next question. "Did the two of you put anything in writing?"

Casey had folded both arms across his chest and was watching her with a slightly amused and all-too-familiar expression. *"Watch your step, young lady."* She could almost hear him growling the words. For a brief moment, she wondered if he might be getting ready to send her to her room the way he had when she was eight. Instead, he gave a not-quite-helpless shrug and answered her question.

"Handshake's always been my bond, little g— Uh, *Logan.* You know that."

"And that was good enough for Mitch?"

"For now. He's been after me to sign this an' that, but . . ."

"But what, Gramps?"

"Haven't got the nitty-gritty worked out just yet, is all."

Thank goodness. "Do you mind if I take a look at the papers?"

"Mercy me, you just can't stop thinkin'. All's you need do is sit down with young Mitch and have yourselves a good gab. Straighten everythin' right out. He's a good lad. You'll see."

"I'm sure he is, Gramps." *A good lad with big plans.* It was those plans that had her worried.

"I'm not too sure he'll be happy to find he's suddenly got another partner, that's all."

Casey didn't answer right away, just gave her a strange sort of look, as if he knew something she didn't.

"Tell you what, little—I mean, *Logan.* You go find yourself somewhere to curl up for a bit. You're lookin' plumb tuckered, you are."

He was right about that. She was more than just tired. Her face felt dry and hot from the sun and wind, she smelled like smoke and lake water, and her jeans had dried stiff and crusty after her close encounter with the shallows of Opakopa. But there was still so much she wanted to know.

"I can rest later, Gramps. Right now, I want—"

"Nope!" He gave the tabletop a gentle thump to make his point. "No arguin'. We might be partners, but don't be forget-tin' who's senior. We'll have a good talk over dinner, you, me, and Mitch. Answer all your questions, I promise. Then, if you're still wantin' to look at them papers, we'll dig 'em up. How's that sound?"

It sounded good. But not half as good as a shower and an hour or two in bed. "Yessir," she said smartly, adding a brisk salute for the senior partner. "But, Gramps?"

He sighed, rolling his eyes, probably expecting another dose of her "hard thinking." "Eh?"

Pushing to her feet, Logan rounded the table, lovingly slip-ping her arms around his neck. "Don't stop calling me Lily, okay? I kinda like it."

The way he moved, so comfortable and confident, anyone would think Mitch Walker already owned the place. Logan sank onto one of the lodge's aging Muskoka chairs and curled her bare legs beneath her, careful to avoid the splinters bristling along the edge of the seat.

She had a headache. The dull, throbbing, unavoidable sort of headache certain to appear after more than fifteen hours of deep, dreamless sleep. Her "partners" hadn't bothered to wake her for dinner. They'd even let her sleep through breakfast. In fact, she'd probably still be sleeping if not for the crew from D'Or-On.

About half an hour earlier, right under her bedroom window, they'd fired up the engine on their four-by-four. For one confusing moment, she'd thought she was back in the city, horns blaring and traffic bustling at all hours of the day and night. Lucky for the noisemakers, and everyone else within earshot, they were long gone by the time she managed to drag herself out of bed. She didn't even want to think about the bone-jarring, seat-numbing trip they'd face, heading back to their camp on the old logging roads that crisscrossed this part of the north. Although, considering the wake-up call they'd provided, maybe a little pain served them right.

She nibbled at her breakfast of toast and jam, tossing the crusts to a chipmunk who disappeared under the front step, then scurried back out to beg for more. ''Sorry, Bud, all gone. Want some coffee?'' The creature sat up and scolded her, beating a hasty retreat when she laughed at his antics.

Feeling utterly abandoned, she sipped her rapidly cooling coffee and turned her attention back to the lake. She'd arrived in the dining room just in time to watch Gramps disappear along the shore, fishing rod in hand. Ruby was nowhere to be found, so instead of enjoying a leisurely catch-up chat over breakfast, she'd carried her toast and coffee outside, counting on a little fresh air to ease the headache and her mood. Thanks to Mitch, her strategy wasn't working.

He was down at the dock, fussing over that airplane of his, sweeping, washing, polishing, as if his life depended on a pair of shiny wings and a floor so clean you could eat off it. A moment ago, he'd disappeared into the boathouse, returning with the first of three passenger seats and the tools to reinstall them in the Beaver's cargo space.

Couldn't that particular task have waited? she wondered, growing more and more annoyed with the man as each minute ticked by. After all, according to the schedule he'd posted in the lodge office, his next charter wasn't until Friday morning—a group of American businessmen up for a weekend of spectacular northern scenery and some of the finest fishing in Canada. Too bad. They'd probably take one look at the place and demand a refund. Or at least a hefty discount. Casey Lodge didn't exactly live up to the brochures these days. Not on the surface, anyway.

She sighed. If Mitch was as gung ho as Gramps seemed to think, as eager to get the place whipped into shape, why wasn't he doing something about the weather-beaten chairs, the half-finished dock, the cabins with peeling walls and leaky roofs?

Why aren't you?

Excellent question, served up with a heaping portion of guilty conscience. Mitch wasn't the one who'd stayed away for nearly ten years. No, he'd been right here, ready, willing, and able whenever Gramps needed a helping hand. So it was nobody's fault but her own that he'd been able to take her rightful place as partner. Thank goodness she hadn't arrived too late to change things.

Logan looked down at the chair's broad armrest, the graceful curve of its seat, absently flicking a chip of forest green paint onto the ground. Had it really been eighteen years since she helped Gramps build the old Muskokas? She remembered that summer as if it were yesterday, the smell of fresh-cut pine, the gentle touch of her grandfather's hand folded over hers, his patience as he taught her how to sand each board until the surface was smooth and clean. Casey's chairs. As much a part of this place as the lake and the loons and the sheltering pines. Her heritage, her responsibility. *Not* Mitch Walker's.

She pushed to her feet, surveying the haphazard row of chairs strung across the patchy bit of lawn in front of the main lodge. Five in all, with another two at each of the six lakeside cabins. Her shoulders ached at the mere thought of all the scraping, sanding, and painting involved, but there was life in the old Muskokas yet, and she aimed to see all seventeen restored to their former glory.

"No time like the present." How many times had Gramps said those very words to her? And *"tomorrow never comes."*

She smiled. Unless he'd rearranged things, there'd be a stiff wire brush in his boathouse workshop, and those old homilies were right on the mark. There'd never be a better time to get started.

Abandoning her empty mug on the arm of the nearest chair, Logan made her way across the scrap of lawn and down the shaded pathway to the lakeshore.

Blanketed with an ever-thickening layer of needles shed by the surrounding trees, the earth underfoot felt soft, almost springy, and each step stirred the woodsy, fresh fragrance of pine. Overhead, beyond the canopy of green, the cloudless morning sky formed an endless dome of cerulean blue. She scanned the horizon and felt a knot of anxiety tighten in her stomach as her gaze settled on a distant haze. *Smoke.*

Her whole body tensed. Heart pounding, fists clenched, her instinctive response was flight. But Logan stood her ground. *Name it. Face it. Overcome it.* She'd lived with this fear for far too long. And, in this case, there truly was nothing to be afraid of. The smudge of smoke on the horizon came from a fire burning hundreds of miles to the west. Andy's fire. He probably had it under control already. If not, he soon would. Nothing ever got the better of Andy Twelvetrees.

She drew a deep breath of sweet, fresh air—not even a hint of smoke—and forced herself to relax. The only danger she faced this morning lived in her own painful memories, in the half-formed recollections that haunted her dreams. It wouldn't be easy, but somehow she'd have to convince Gramps to help her remember and face the fears. After all, a person couldn't hope to spend a lifetime in the north without encountering a forest fire now and again.

From somewhere along the shore came the melancholy cry of a loon, and Logan smiled to hear her grandfather's echoing call. She was tempted to join him, try fishing for her lunch the way she had in the old days. The lure of the lake was almost irresistible, but the sight of Mitch's floatplane bobbing gently on the water as he toiled inside reminded her of the task she'd set for herself.

Part of her hoped he'd emerge from the plane before she reached the boathouse, give her a reason to stop and talk, do a little of that ''getting acquainted'' Gramps had encouraged.

She hesitated on the beach, rolling a stone under the sole of her blue canvas deck shoe as she eyed the floatplane. The memory of her last close encounter with Mitch, caught up in his arms as he kept the two of them balanced on the edge of that rickety old dock, was disturbingly fresh in her mind. She could still feel the warmth of his chest beneath her palms, his easy laughter rumbling through her.

She pictured him, moments ago, lugging that seat from the boathouse and into the plane, his muscles straining under a snug white T-shirt. Glancing down at her pale arms and positively pasty bare legs, she recalled his healthy, sun-drenched tan and felt horribly citified.

That did it. She wouldn't confront him now. Better to have their first heart-to-heart up in the lodge. Here at the dock he had his floatplane, his ''Old Beauty,'' for backup—a definite home court advantage. The man might not be so annoyingly self-confident in the dining room. And maybe she wouldn't feel so annoyingly intimidated by him. Nudging the stone one last time, she turned and made a dash for the boathouse.

It took several seconds for her eyes to adjust to the dim interior. Sunlight filtered through mullioned panes of grimy, yellowed glass. Dust motes hung in the warm, musty air and a peaceful silence wrapped her in an almost palpable cloak of memories.

The old boathouse had always been her refuge, her secret place. How many times had she abandoned her chores in favor of a lazy afternoon, curled up in the bottom of one of Gramps's fishing boats with a favorite book and a handful of cookies fresh from Ruby's pantry? She'd always been so certain she was hidden from prying eyes, safe from interruptions. But now, from her grown-up vantage point near the door, she knew Gramps would've seen her if he'd bothered to peek inside. The thought that he must have known, and had chosen to keep her secret, filled her with a rush of warmth and love for the old man. It was long past time to start paying him back for a lifetime of affection.

She moved slowly past the gently bobbing row of boats moored one behind the other in the dark water. Two shiny new Lunds sat nearest the door, top-of-the-line fishing craft and the first clear sign that Gramps might be right about a return to prosperity for the lodge. Behind them, like poor relations wearing faded hand-me-downs, were the boats she and Gramps, and sometimes Andy, had used to fish and explore Thembi's waters when she was growing up. Six in all, with a seventh cradled for repairs in Gramps's workshop. Despite their age, each and every one of them looked well kept, clean, and ready to go. Maybe the old man was right. Maybe things were looking up around here.

Her spirits buoyed, Logan rummaged in the drawers under Casey's workbench, collecting a stiff wire brush, a paint scraper, and several sheets of sandpaper. By the end of the afternoon she'd have at least two of those old chairs ready for a fresh coat of paint. But was there any on hand to do the job?

She made a quick check of the cupboards and overhead shelves. Nothing. But if Mitch had such big plans for sprucing the place up, he'd have been certain to lay in a supply of paint and wood stain. . . .

''What's up?''

Logan jumped at the sound of his voice. It seemed a little too loud, somehow. A little too confident. She barely managed to hang onto the wire brush and scraper. The sandpaper fluttered to the floor as she turned to face him.

''Sorry. Didn't mean to frighten you.'' Mitch pulled off his sunglasses, hooked them into the collar of his T-shirt, then folded his arms across his chest.

"You d-didn't," she sputtered, uncomfortably aware of the hot blush that marked her face. He'd asked a simple, friendly question, surely not intended to make her uneasy. So why did she suddenly feel like a trespasser? *Get over it!*

"Okay, maybe you did startle me. A little. I was just . . . daydreaming. Reminiscing. This used to be my favorite spot."

"Yeah." Mitch nodded, easing into a comfortable slouch, his back against the doorjamb. His knowing gaze slipped away from her face, coming to rest on one of the dowdy old boats. "It's real good when you need a quiet spot."

His tone was almost reverent, full of warmth and affection for the place. Maybe Gramps was right about him after all. And it was certain she'd never have a better opportunity to catch him off guard.

"So, what's this I hear about you and Gramps being partners?"

His gaze flickered briefly in her direction, then settled once more on the gently rocking fishing boats. Was he worried? Afraid she might put an end to his big plans? If he was, it sure didn't show.

"I dunno, Logan." He shifted slightly, crossing his feet at the ankles, sliding his hands into the deep pockets of his jeans. "Suppose you fill me in. What did you hear?"

Was he kidding? No. Not kidding. He was watching her now, his expression guarded and strangely unsettling. He probably thought she'd back down. Well, he had another think coming. She tossed the wire brush and scraper onto the workbench, turning back to face him with her hands planted firmly on her hips.

"Gramps says you two are partners. He also says you want him to sign some papers."

His frown deepened. "Yeah. So what's your point?"

"My *point?*" Logan bit back the rest of her retort. After four years with a class of wily teenagers, Mitch's game plan was all too familiar—get Teach mad and she'll forget about the lesson. *Not this time!*

"Just that it doesn't look like a place with a new, *active* partner. It was pretty much of a shock to find things so run-down." *There. Let's see him explain that!*

"A shock? How do you think I feel? The way Casey talked about his granddaughter, I thought Lily was just a little kid."

Did this guy take lessons in changing the subject? "Afraid not. Gramps might not want to believe it, but I'm all grown up now. And, more important, I'm home to stay."

Mitch greeted the announcement with a blank stare.

"What's wrong? Afraid I'll spoil your big plans?"

His eyebrows arched ever so slightly. "What plans would those be?"

"You tell me."

"Y'know, Logan, I think you should be having this conversation with your grandfather, not me."

"I already did. He told me you've only known each other since last fall. Pretty quick partnership, I'd say."

"Now wait just a darned minute."

Mitch straightened abruptly and strode toward her. Logan held her ground. She wasn't about to let him bully her.

"You've only got that partly right," he said, parking himself in front of her, toe-to-toe and obviously irritated.

"Oh, yeah?"

"Yeah. I started flying charters into the lodge last fall. But I've known your grandfather for a *lot* longer than that. Used to fly his supply runs . . . sometimes I'd stick around and go fishing . . . help him out with this or that. It's a lot for one man to handle. And Casey's not as young as he used to be, you know."

"Not as old as I'm gonna be, either, young fella!"

Mitch groaned, turning toward the doorway red-faced and muttering a hasty apology.

"Pffft!" Casey waved him off. "Figured you two'd be catchin' a few winks after yesterday. But since you're not tuckered out, me an' Ruby got a bit of a job for you." He winked slyly. "Just the thing for a couple of new partners. Give you a chance to practice at gettin' along."

Chapter Six

"Berry pie." The old man licked his lips as if he could taste it already. "Got Ruby makin' pastry. Now all's we need is some ripe, red berries."

Logan stifled a groan. If Gramps had waited another few minutes, she might have pried a little truth out of Mitch. But after that "new partners" comment, he was certain to be on guard.

"Isn't it a bit early for raspberries, Gramps?"

"Nope." He ambled into the boathouse, stopping to rummage in a pile of crates that cluttered the corner. "Been snackin' on 'em for near a week now, here an' there. Unless I miss my guess, today's the day, little girl. Trick is to get 'em before the bears do."

Turning, the old man dropped a nest of weather-beaten baskets on the floor at her feet. "Listen up, now. You're headin' east along the lakeshore. Mitch, you know the spot . . . where that lightnin' strike cleared everythin' out 'bout four years back. Them berries love the meadowland."

Mitch nodded wordlessly, wearing a woebegone expression. Apparently, spending a pleasant morning in the woods with his new partner wasn't on his list of favorite things to do. Maybe pumping bilge water out of one of the old boats would be more to his liking.

"But, Gramps, I was planning to scrape down the chairs this morning. And Mitch has another seat to install—"

"Pffft! Y'got all summer for scrapin', little girl. But them berries won't wait!" He turned away, leaning heavily on his cane as he made his way through the door. Before he rounded the corner, Casey stopped to offer one last piece of advice. "Don't be eatin' all Ruby's pie fillin' on the way back, now. Y'hear?"

Logan sighed.

"Not easy saying no to your Gramps, is it?"

"That's for sure." She looked up to find Mitch studying her, his gloomy mood of a moment ago replaced by a slightly bemused smile.

He flipped the nest of baskets into the air with the toe of his boot, catching them on the fly and passing two to Logan. "Guess we'd better hustle. Unless you don't like Ruby's pies . . ."

Logan grinned. She'd never met anyone who didn't like Ruby's pies. And truth be told, she could think of a lot worse ways to spend a warm June morning than going berry picking with Mitch Walker. *Time for a truce.* "Bet I can fill two baskets faster than you."

Mitch snagged the dark glasses from his collar, settling them firmly on his nose once more. "Pretty sure of yourself, aren't you, Logan?"

"For a city girl, you mean?"

"No, for someone I'm willing to bet hasn't picked wild berries in a *very* long time."

She shrugged. "Hardly something you forget."

"Okay. You're on. What do I get if I win?"

"Oh, I don't know. What did you have in mind?" *Big mistake!* Logan didn't wait for his response, striding purposefully out of the boathouse, across the narrow, rocky beach, and onto the lakeside trail. She was well out of sight of the lodge before Mitch caught up, matching his pace to hers as he fell into step beside her.

What did you have in mind? Why on earth had she said that? Imagining what his answer might be brought a warmth to her cheeks that had nothing to do with the bright morning sun. He was watching, she could almost feel his gaze. Those wonderful, warm blue eyes.

Standing toe-to-toe with him back in the boathouse, she'd searched those eyes and found nothing but honest emotion. Enough to cause a brief twinge of shame for doubting his motives.

''You already owe me one, you know.''

Startled, as much by the nearness of him as by his unexpected announcement, she blurted out a flustered reply. ''Owe? I— One, what? What are you talking about?''

''Yesterday's challenge. Had something to do with cold water, didn't it? And *you* ducked out on me.''

Logan walked a bit faster, forcing herself to watch the path ahead. It was overgrown with weeds and saplings, littered with fallen branches and gnarled roots, all of them lying in wait for an unwary hiker. The last thing she wanted was to wind up sprawled on her face in front of Mitch. She didn't need to look back at him to know he was already smiling. She'd heard it in his voice . . . the same sort of playful grin he'd worn yesterday when he'd held her in his arms on the dock.

''Soooo . . . I win, you pay up.''

''You've gotta be kidding!'' She stopped short, ducking out of his way just in time to avoid a collision. ''You *really* want to throw me into the lake?''

He leaned close, eyebrows raised above the rims of his glasses. ''Not afraid of a little cold water, are you?''

Logan matched his grin. Thought he could use her own words against her, did he? Strangely enough, she was starting to enjoy his little game and it was *definitely* time to raise the stakes. ''What happens if I win?''

''If you win?'' He chuckled, obviously certain he had no

worries in that department. "Logan, if you win . . . the debt is forgiven."

"I don't think so. Let's say if I win . . . *you* take the plunge."

"Deal!"

Not a moment's hesitation. And he'd already taken the lead, moving briskly along the narrow track, setting a pace with his long-legged stride that left her jogging to keep up. She was *really* going to enjoy dunking him.

"So, how . . . how far is this . . . berry patch?"

"What's the matter? Can't keep up?" Mitch flashed a grin, looking back at her over his shoulder without slowing down. "Thought you city types liked running. I hear you even do it for fun."

"Yeah, well, that . . . that's difrent." *No roots to trip on or logs to leap.* "And I'll keep . . . up . . . just fine."

He chuckled, slowing his pace to a more comfortable walk. "It's just around the lake a bit. Should be able to follow the path most of the way."

This far from the lodge, the trail was narrow and winding, a serpentine track along the lakeshore, cutting inland at irregular intervals to bypass rocky outcroppings or dense thickets of bramble and brush. The gentle lapping of water against rock and the chatter of jays overhead kept them company—sounds of home for Logan, joined, whenever the breeze died, by the lazy drone of the season's first hatch of mosquitos.

It seemed a shame to break the peaceful mood with more questions about Mitch's plans for the lodge. There'd be plenty of time for that later. For now, she'd simply enjoy the day, set her pace to follow a few yards behind him, and let the forest soothe her soul.

But as they walked, Logan found her gaze drawn not to the surrounding woodland, but to the broad shoulders and strong back of the new and perplexing man in her life. She pondered the easy rhythm of his stride, the patterns of dappled sunlight dancing across his white T-shirt, the dark curl of hair at the nape of his neck . . . that's what was different! He'd had a haircut. No big deal, just enough to tame the wildness. *But I liked him wild.*

The thought both surprised and frightened her. After all, she knew next to nothing about him. Yet something, some sense or intuition, kept insisting she should trust him—with Gramps, the lodge, her future—but not necessarily with finding the berry patch! Did he really have a clue where he was going?

Mitch broke into a whistle before she could voice the question. It was a loud and not-quite-melodious tune that could only mean one thing—the meadow was nearby. Whistling was one of Gramps's old tricks—let the bears know you're coming and they'll clear out before you arrive. She felt a brief twinge of jealously to think her grandfather had spent the last few years passing down his love and understanding of these woods to Mitch instead of to her, but she brushed it off. She'd grown up with Gramps as her tutor. The old man's love of nature had been her inspiration for a career in science and teaching. It was a legacy she intended to pass on to a new generation, kids whose idea of wildlife meant hanging out on Yonge Street on a Saturday night. And if that interfered with Mitch Walker and his big plans . . . well, he'd just have to adjust.

Moments later the sheltered trail gave way to open meadow, a tangle of grass and sedges, marred by a handful of blackened tree stumps . . . all that remained of the lightning-struck forest. Logan half expected to see a moose or two grazing on the new growth, but Mitch's whistling had warned away more than just black bears. The tract was empty.

"Looks like Casey was right again." Mitch dropped to one knee as he spoke and, after only a moment's work, produced a handful of plump, perfect berries. He popped them into his mouth and grinned up at her. "Wouldn't want you to accuse me of taking a head start."

"Hey, you probably need one!"

Laughing, Logan made a dash for the lake. Gramps always said you'd find the biggest berries on the plants that kept their feet wet. *Right again.* After only twenty minutes of picking, she'd more than half-filled one of her baskets . . . and eaten almost as many along the way.

"Hey! I was beginning to think the bears had got you. Don't you know any better than to disappear like that?"

Logan tensed. The jays overhead, even the crickets at her feet, had fallen silent at Mitch's approach, as if they, too, resented the intrusion. But tempering the obvious annoyance in his voice was an undercurrent of relief. Hearing it, Logan let her sharp retort die unspoken.

He was right, of course. She did know better. She shouldn't have wandered away from the berry patch without telling him. But she'd needed the last few moments of solitude, and had hoped to find them without the painful explanations he was certain to want. There was no avoiding them now.

"Logan?" His hand brushed her arm. "Hey, you all right?"

No. Not all right. Her throat tightened, cutting off the reply she would have whispered. How could she face him? If she turned around now, he'd know she'd been crying.

"Look, I . . . I didn't mean to scare you, honest. Just can't seem to stop sneaking up on you today. What is this place, anyway?" He nudged at the crumbling foundation with the toe of his boot. "Not much left of it."

Just memories. If only she hadn't caught a glimpse of ruined chimney through the trees. If only she'd listened to her own advice and stayed at the lakeshore. But, no. She'd followed her heart, not her head, drawn by an overwhelming need to see the old place again. A place she'd thought lived only in her dreams. And her nightmares.

"Logan?" As if sensing her pain, Mitch moved closer, resting his hands on her shoulders. "What's wrong? Are you hurt?"

"No." She shook her head, ignoring the single tear that trickled down her cheek. "It . . . it's just this place."

She looked down at the old stone foundation, decayed and overgrown with weeds, then reached out to touch the worn granite of the chimney. Not much left.

"It used to be . . . home." The words rode a wave of emotion that threatened to sweep her away. *Hang on.* Pressing her palm against the sun-warmed stone, she steadied her breathing and stilled her thoughts, drawing strength from the past.

"Fire?"

Fire! The word left her breathless, fighting a too-familiar feeling of panic . . . the same feeling that came in her nightmares. The same feeling she'd had yesterday and again this morning, when she'd seen that smoke on the horizon. How could she possibly face her fears, if she couldn't even give them a name? *Name it. Face it. Overcome it!* Time to follow her own good advice.

"F-fire." She nodded, swiping the tear away. "A long time ago. I don't . . . can't really remember. I was just a kid. . . ."

"You're trembling."

"I am?" She looked down at her hands, surprised to discover he was right. But his hands felt steady and warm, first on her shoulders, now sliding down the length of her arms, so gentle and comforting. If she moved just a little closer, her head would touch his chest, her head would find his shoulder, and his arms would close around her, sheltering and strong. She remembered that moment on the dock, how completely safe she'd felt in his embrace. If only . . .

Too soon! Pulling away, she turned to look up at him with a forced and faltering smile. This was no time to fall for a pair of strong arms and a gentle voice. Far too much was at stake.

She had to be sure of him, certain she could trust him, before
. . . *Don't even think it!*

"It's nothing. Just a lot of old ghosts." There. At least she'd
managed to keep the tremble out of her voice.

Mitch said nothing, only nodded, but his eyes held a depth
of understanding Logan hadn't expected and was far from ready
to confront. She gulped a deep breath and tore her gaze away,
scuffing at the earth with the toe of her shoe while mentally
scrambling to safety. "Aren't you afraid?"

He frowned, playing thoughtfully with the sunglasses dangling from his collar. "Afraid of what? Your ghosts?"

"No . . ." She stepped slowly away, watching as he shoved
his hands into his pockets, missing the feel of them on her shoulders. "Of losing the bet!"

She took off at a run before Mitch could answer. Too many
dark memories lingered in the ruins of that cabin, ghosts of the
past, shrouded in sadness and fear, crowding her, demanding to
be heard. Back at the berry patch, she'd be able to push them
out of her mind, concentrate on filling those baskets and winning
the bet. If it wasn't already too late. While she'd been wasting
time, he'd probably filled one basket and half of another . . . and
she still hadn't topped up the first.

Nearly an hour later, Logan was still picking raspberries, her
fingers stained red with juice, arms and legs scratched and itchy
from too many close encounters with the spiny canes of the
plants. Not to mention at least a dozen mosquito bites.

She and Mitch had kept up a constant conversation across the
meadow as they worked and, by bits and pieces, Logan had
heard all his plans for the new dock at Casey Lodge. It would
be big enough to moor two floatplanes—the Beaver and a new
Twin Otter he dreamed of adding to the *AirWalker* fleet in the
not-too-distant future—as well as all of Casey's fishing boats.

Listening to him talk, she couldn't help but share his enthusiasm and began to think Gramps might be right about him, after all.

Eventually, they'd given up hollering back and forth across the distance and Mitch had started whistling again. The sound reminded her of something, but . . . oh, yeah . . . fingernails on a blackboard. She snickered quietly. It was safe to assume there wouldn't be any bears within earshot of *that.* And nice to know the man had at least one serious fault, despite what Gramps had to say about his many talents and virtues.

The bear-chasing whistle grew closer, stopping abruptly as the toes of Mitch's work boots entered her range of vision. Logan glanced sideways at her two nearly full baskets and laughed softly to herself. "Better get busy. These plants are loaded . . . I'll be ahead of you in no time."

"Uh . . . Logan?"

"Hmm?" She lifted a leaf, pulled off another cluster of fat, juicy berries, and dropped them into a basket before looking up. *Uh-oh.* Things were *not* going according to plan.

Grinning, Mitch placed his two baskets on the ground beside hers. Both were full to overflowing with ripe raspberries. One rolled off the top of the heap and landed beside her.

"Keep it," he said dryly, nudging the fallen berry toward her with the toe of his boot. "I do believe I won."

Chapter Seven

"You might want to take your shoes off before you pay up. It's a long walk back to the lodge and, well, I'd *hate* to think of you having to slosh all the way."

The easy smile Logan had found so endearing yesterday morning danced across Mitch's features once again as she grasped his outstretched hand and let him pull her to her feet. His fingers felt cool against her skin and she shivered, anticipating the shock of cold water she'd soon encounter. Somehow, sloshing seemed like the least of her worries.

Shrugging, she grinned back at him, hoping she looked a lot more nonchalant than she felt. "Wouldn't be the first time."

"Oh? Lost a lot of bets, have you?"

"No. Picked a lot of berries. And sometimes the mosquitoes would get *so* thick..." She laughed at the memory, thankful once more for the morning's gentle breeze that, so far, had kept most of the biting insects at bay. "Didn't matter *how* cold the water was, Andy and I used to spend as much time splashing around in the lake as we did filling our baskets."

"You and Andy, eh?" A hint of something dangerous flashed in his eyes as his smile flickered briefly. "Okay. But did Andy do *this*?"

Logan's next breath ended in a whoop of surprise as Mitch scooped her into his arms, effortlessly lifting her off her feet. Instinct sent her arms twining around his neck, but it was thoughts of an impending bath in Thembi's frigid water that kept her hanging on. She might have to pay up, but she didn't have to make it easy on him.

"Hey! Okay, okay. You don't have to strangle me." He regarded her skeptically, then set her gently on her feet again, keeping one arm locked firmly around her waist.

She held on. It felt so natural to leave her arms around his neck. Unquestionably safer, too. He was a lot less likely to dunk her if he couldn't pry her loose. Not that she was trying to weasel out of their bet or anything. No way! Just making things a little more interesting, was all.

"You don't have to worry, Mitch, I . . . I . . ."

With each word she spoke, Mitch seemed to lean closer, tilting his head, watching, considering, until she felt as if all his attention and every fiber of his being were focused directly on her. His mouth curved into a gentle smile, drawing her gaze and scrambling her thoughts. When he caught his bottom lip between his teeth, she found herself wondering how a kiss might feel, how it might taste. Like raspberries, if he'd eaten as many as she had. . . .

What are you doing? This was no time to think about kissing him, no matter how tempting the thought might be. If she kissed him, she'd forget all about those questions she'd intended to ask, and forgetting was the last thing she wanted. Gramps and the lodge were a lot more important than a stolen kiss from a man she'd only known for a day and a half. No matter how intriguing.

His lips parted. He looked at her intently. "You were saying . . . ?"

I was?

His smile grew playful, almost as if he knew the effect he was having on her. Maybe he did. Yesterday, she'd been certain he knew her thoughts, but now . . . *Let's hope not!*

She looked away. His lips were none of her business, no matter how warm or soft or downright fascinating those lips might be. Forcing herself to focus on his equally fascinating chest, on the expanse of hard muscle hidden away under the soft white cotton of his T-shirt, Logan tried to concentrate on exactly what it was that Mitch didn't need to worry about.

"I, um . . . I was saying . . . Well, you know, a bet's a bet. You won fair and square." *Oh, great! When in doubt, spout a few clichés!* She sucked in a deep breath. "You can let go. I'm *not* planning on ducking out on you again."

He laughed, a deep, low chuckle that made the T-shirt shiver against his skin. "The thought never occurred to me."

Was it her imagination, or was he holding her even closer now? No, not imagination. Mere inches from her face, those cotton-covered muscles rose and fell with each breath he took. And she wasn't imagining the fact that her arms were still wrapped around his neck, either. She loosened her hold, let her hands trail slowly over his shoulders to settle in the center of his chest. *Now what?* Apparently Mitch wasn't about to release her, but unless she could put some space between them there was simply nowhere else to put her hands.

"You," he said, in a voice that reminded her of warm honey, "feel a bit overheated."

No kidding! Of course, his sultry voice and the strong, steady beat of his heart beneath her palms had nothing at all to do with it. Nothing at all. She'd spent the last hour picking raspberries in full sun by the lakeshore while he'd stayed on the shady side of the meadow. No wonder his skin felt so cool. She shivered again.

"Too much sun?" Gently, Mitch brushed her cheek with his fingertips, tracing a line down her neck, over her shoulder, onto the sun-warmed flesh of her arm. His smile slowly faded. "We'd better get back."

Logan's hands drifted slowly to her sides as he stepped away. *Too much sun?* What on earth was he thinking? *"Poor little city girl, can't take a morning's work outdoors."* Couldn't he at least give her credit for being smart enough to use a sunscreen?

"I'm fine." She scowled. "What's the matter? Afraid I might splash some of that cold water on you?"

Mitch stared at her in slack-jawed surprise. Biting back a laugh, Logan finished the challenge, "Who's ducking out now?"

"Not ducking, just choosing my time. More fun if you're not expecting it, don't you think?"

Oh, wonderful! She tried not to gape at him, imagining the countless opportunities he'd have to send her, unsuspecting, into the lake. "Huh. For you, maybe."

"Well, that's what winning's all about, right?" Grinning, he reached for his baskets, tipping some of the fruit into hers until all four were equally full. "Besides, if we don't hurry back, Ruby won't have time to make those pies before dinner. Don't know about you, but I don't want to be responsible for Casey's bad mood if he doesn't get his dessert!"

She couldn't argue with that. Apparently he knew her grandfather pretty well. She could only hope the old man knew as much about his new partner. Hoisting the baskets, she hurried across the meadow, catching up to Mitch as they entered the shady forest path.

"Tell me about D'Or-On."

Mitch fired a glance over his shoulder, too brief for her to read his expression, but the slight hesitation in his stride, the sudden tension in his shoulders, suggested the question had taken him by surprise.

"Not much to tell. They're doing a lot of claim staking to the north of us. There's been talk about gold, rumors about a big strike, but that's a lot farther west, out beyond the fire." He shrugged. "Who knows? It's all speculation so far. Your Gramps is real happy about the new business they're sending our way, though."

"Yeah, so he said. But what about you?"

His shoulders tensed again. "What about me?"

Logan sighed. This would be so much easier if only she could see his face. Her students had never been able to fool her about missing assignments or unauthorized absences. All she'd had to do was study their faces to know the truth. Mitch Walker's broad back was a whole lot better at keeping secrets. The only thing she knew for sure was that he hadn't appreciated the questions.

"Look, I'm not trying to pick a fight. You said Gramps is happy, and I agree. It's just, well, you didn't sound so happy about it yourself. If there's a problem, I'd like to know."

Mitch stopped, turning slowly to face her, studying her for a long, awkward moment before he replied. "If somebody wanted to, it'd be pretty easy to take advantage of Casey."

My thought, exactly. "How?"

"He's too trusting. Thinks everybody's word is their bond."

"And you don't?"

"You *do?*"

Mitch regarded her for a moment, then wheeled abruptly and strode off along the path. As she hurried to catch up, Logan pondered the cryptic expression he'd been wearing just before he turned away. Had he interpreted her question as an insult to his integrity? Or was he more convinced than ever that this bothersome city girl was incredibly naive? Both, probably.

"Mitch, I didn't mean . . ."

"Yes, you did. And I can't say I blame you. I mean, why *should* you trust me? You don't know me. You weren't expecting to come home and find a stranger in partnership with your grandfather . . . a partnership you wanted for yourself."

He halted again, so unexpectedly this time that Logan nearly ran into him. Without turning to face her, he added quietly, "So, tell me . . . should I be looking for a new job?"

How did he do that? Once again he'd managed to turn the

subject away from Gramps and D'Or-On without telling her anything she didn't already know. What was he trying to hide?

She stared at the broad expanse of white cotton between his shoulder blades and considered her next move. It was obvious that confrontation and direct questions would get her nowhere. Maybe it was time to try a new tack. Hadn't Gramps always said you could catch more flies with honey than with vinegar?

"You're right. I've got no reason to trust you. Yet. But I *do* trust my grandfather. He might not do business by the book, but he must have good reasons to want you for a partner. So, unless you have some objection, I guess we're a threesome." *There. Deal with that!*

"Right. A threesome."

Once again, as he strode away from her, Logan found herself wishing she could see Mitch's face. Apart from his brief acknowledgment, he offered no response to her peace offering and his broad, muscular back gave no hint of what his reaction had been. Why wouldn't he look her in the eye? Was the thought of having her for a partner really so repulsive? Surely it wasn't the "city girl" thing again . . . or was it?

She trailed along the path behind him, keeping silent until she couldn't bear the tension between them any longer. Why did she suddenly feel she had to justify herself to him?

Because, like it or not, Mitch Walker isn't the newcomer here. You are.

"Listen, Mitch, I figure I've got just as much to prove as you have. Not only to you, but to my grandfather as well. Maybe we could just give it a try for a while. For his sake. What do you think?"

His shoulders seemed to relax a bit, but still Mitch kept silent, striding purposefully along the narrow, winding pathway, head down, as if lost in his own thoughts. Had he even heard what she'd said? Right now, the man seemed oblivious, not only to her but to the beauty of the forest around them. If only he'd stop for a minute, stand quietly beside her, let the scents and sounds of the woodland soothe him. Then, maybe, he'd notice the effect this place had on her. Already she felt more mellow than she had in months. Surely it showed. Surely he'd see that she wasn't just a city girl, that she really belonged here.

But his dogged pace didn't slow, and wishing wouldn't make him turn around.

"My stars!" Smoothing the front of her apron with flour-dusted hands, Ruby Twelvetrees examined the brimming baskets Logan and Mitch had deposited on her spotless kitchen counter.

"Look at 'em all! Enough to feed an army. Now, don't tell me you two didn't know our last guests left this morning. It'll be just the four of us for suppers till the end of the week. And even Casey can't eat *that* much raspberry pie." She winked at Logan, adding, "Guess you'll just have to help me put the rest in the freezer, eh?"

"Sure, Ruby. No problem." Logan forced a smile. It would be the perfect opportunity for that long talk they'd missed out on last night. And if anybody knew what Mitch Walker had to hide, and why, it would be Ruby. The older woman was studying him now, wearing an understanding and thoughtful expression.

Logan chanced a sideways glance at her unwilling partner. He'd maintained his icy silence all the way back to the lodge and stood beside her now, hands shoved deep into his pockets. He was staring out the window, shifting awkwardly from one foot to the other, as if he couldn't wait to make his escape.

"Hungry?" asked Ruby, turning her knowing gaze on Logan. "Made a chicken salad for Casey. Leftovers are in the fridge." Lifting one of the berry baskets, she turned to the sink and began rinsing the fruit. "Help yourselves if you want lunch."

"I'm still too full of raspberries to think about eating anything. Maybe later, though. How about you, Mitch?"

She smiled up at him. Let him sulk if that's what he wanted, but she didn't have to join him in his gloomy mood. Like it or not, they were partners. At least for a little while. And the sooner he relaxed and accepted the inevitability of it all, the better. For both of them.

"Yeah. Maybe later. I've got work to do." His gaze locked briefly with hers before he bolted out the door, acknowledging her bewildered expression with a terse phrase as the screen slammed shut behind him. "We'll talk later."

Count on it.

"Well, I declare!" said Ruby, reaching for a second basket of fruit. "What on earth's gotten into him?"

"Beats me." Logan carried the last two baskets to the sink and nudged Ruby aside. "I'll wash, you bake."

"Just like the old days, eh, child? Don't tell me they didn't teach you how to cook at those fancy schools!"

"Hey, I always figured if *you* couldn't make me into a passable cook, nobody could. So . . . I took wood shop, instead."

"You did?" Ruby beamed at her in obvious delight. "Well, good for you, child. Good for you." She stopped measuring berries long enough to poke Logan with her elbow and ask in a conspiratorial whisper, "How'd you ever manage to slip that past your Auntie Pearl?"

"You're kidding, right?"

Ruby shook her head.

"All Pearl ever wanted was to get me into the 'right' schools. She didn't much care what I did once I got there. Unless my grades started to slip, that is. Then it was lecture time." She groaned at the memory. "Ever heard one of Pearl's long-distance lectures?"

"No, can't say as I have. Watched your granddaddy react to a few of 'em, though." She chuckled. "Never saw such a performance in all my life—rollin' his eyes, wavin' his hands— poor man couldn't get a word in edgewise."

Logan giggled. "Poor Gramps. He put up with a lot on my account, didn't he?"

"Huh! Child, if you ask me, *you* were the one doin' all the puttin' up." Ruby gave her a dark, sorrowful glance. "All those years away from home . . ."

"Now, Ruby . . ."

"No! It was wrong, sendin' you away. Only thing your granddaddy and me ever disagreed on."

Ruby had been rummaging in a drawer while she spoke and slammed it sharply now, as if to make her point. Clutched in her plump right hand was an oversized wooden spoon. She used it to jab at the air a couple of times, muttering "stubborn old man" and a few other choice phrases.

Logan concentrated on washing the last of the berries. It was either that or laugh out loud at Ruby's antics. The way she remembered it, Ruby and Gramps were always squabbling over one thing or another. Of course, it had always been good-natured. She hated the thought that she might have been re-sponsible, even indirectly, for a serious disagreement between the two people she loved most in the world.

She watched as the older woman measured sugar and sprin-kled tapioca onto the berries, gently stirring the mixture with the old wooden spoon. It had to be the same one she'd used for baking fifteen years ago. It had looked rustic and time-worn back then, too, a relic from her grandfather's past, just like the old rocking chair in the corner, the often-bleached white tile countertop, the chipped enamel on the edge of the old-fashioned sink, the scuffed but spotless red linoleum. Once again, Logan felt as if nothing had changed, as if she'd never been away. Or maybe time had stood still, waiting for her to return.

Gazing contentedly out the window, she saw the same trees, only bigger, the same rocks she'd played on as a child, the same beautiful lake. *No.* Her gaze settled on Mitch's floatplane. Not everything had stayed the same.

"How well do you know him, Ruby?"

"Who's that, child?"

"Mitch. Is he always so hard to get along with?"

"Hard to—"

Abruptly, Ruby turned away, busying herself wiping raspberry juice off the counter. But if Logan wasn't mistaken, the woman was laughing, her plump shoulders and hips jiggling gently. What the heck was so funny?

After a moment, Ruby gave an audible, if muffled, snicker. "Oh, my." Shaking her head, she began to fill the pie shells with the prepared filling. "Our Mitch, hard to get along with? No, I wouldn't say that."

"Well, what *would* you say about him? Who is he? Where'd he come from? Can we trust him?"

"Never given me a reason not to. Guess I'd say he seems like an honorable man. Sure has done a lot to help your granddaddy." She paused, thoughtful. "Y'know, I've always felt there was something he wanted to talk about. Something . . ."

"What?"

Ruby frowned and shook her head, then began weaving a lattice top of pastry for one of the pies. "I shouldn't gossip."

"Aw, c'mon, Ruby. Not you, too. Gramps has changed the subject on me every time I've asked him about Mitch. And this morning . . . well, except for his plans for the new dock, I don't know anything more about him than I did yesterday."

"Would you want me telling your secrets, sayin' why I think you do things?" Ruby didn't wait for a response. "No. 'Course not. Don't be so impatient, child. You've just barely met the man. Take your time, get to know him. You might be glad of it."

Logan was tempted to argue the point, but deep down she knew Ruby was right. As partners, they'd have all the time in the world to get to know each other.

She worked quietly for a time, rinsing and sorting the ripe, juicy raspberries, readying them for the freezer. Some wintry afternoon, Ruby would surprise them with a taste of summer sunshine—a fresh-baked pie or maybe a strudel, another of Gramps's special favorites.

"All done," she said at last. "Want me to pack them?"

"No, you can leave that to me. Why don't you go have a visit with your granddaddy. Maybe he'll answer some of those questions you're so full of."

"He looks so frail, Ruby. Should I be worried about him?"

"Frail? Better not let *him* hear that! No, child, he's just older, that's all. Same as all of us. Got a bit of arthritis in his hip and it pains him sometimes, but he's still a fine, strong man. Too darned stubborn to be anything else!"

Logan let her breath out in a long sigh. "That's the best news I've had in ages. Where is he, anyway? We didn't see him when we came up from the lake."

"Well . . . after lunch he went off to work on the plumbing in that new cabin he's building next to number six. Don't suppose he's had a chance to tell you about that, has he?"

"No, he hasn't. Why am I not surprised?"

Ruby didn't have to answer. The cryptic little smile on her face said it all. "I think I saw him coming up the path a while ago." She looked up at the clock and nodded. "Um-hmm. Sometimes takes a nap about now. Why don't you go on upstairs and see?"

"I think I'll do that." She breathed a frustrated sigh. "Maybe I'll get lucky and catch him talking in his sleep." Something told her it was the only way she was ever going to get any answers.

Chapter Eight

Give it a try for a while. For his sake.

Mitch let the lid of his toolbox slam shut, locking it into place with a quick, impatient motion. Why did she have to be so bang-on right?

Slouching onto the newly installed passenger seat, he propped both feet on the back of the seat ahead and wearily closed his eyes.

Pond scum. Swamp gas. No, one of those slimy bottom feeders. Couldn't get much lower, and that was exactly how he felt. Whether or not Logan Paris had what it would take to make the lodge and their ill-conceived partnership work, she at least had the guts to give it a try. She'd taken the first step, shown she was willing. And what had he done about it?

Nothing. Nada. Zip. Zilch. She'd probably added arrogant, rude, and obnoxious to her list of complaints about him. And rightfully so. He could've acknowledged her offer with something more than a grunt, maybe agreed to give it a try. But no. Much as he hated to admit it, Logan Paris, the city girl, had him on the run.

City girl? Even thinking the words embarrassed him now. She was no girl, she was a woman. Strong, confident, passionate about life and about this place. It was difficult to imagine her failing at anything she set her mind to. Why, even though she'd lost that stupid bet this morning, *she* was the one who'd wound up looking good, taking it with grace and style, ready to face the consequences, too. Maybe he should've collected right then and there, kept the upper hand instead of . . .

No. He could still feel the warmth of her as she leaned against him, the gentle, hesitant touch of her hands. He remembered the scent of her hair, the lilt of her voice. And her lips. Tossing her into the lake had been the farthest thing from his mind. He'd just wanted to hold her, and he'd been so close to stealing a kiss, so certain she wanted him to try.

Huh! Dream on. What made him think a woman like her needed protecting? Or that she could ever be interested in someone like him? If her grandfather hadn't saddled her with the partnership, she wouldn't have spared him a second glance. And who could blame her? What did a backwoods bush pilot have to offer an educated, independent woman like Logan Paris?

The best darned business partner she's ever likely to find, that's what.

His feet hit the floorboards with a thud, setting the plane in motion. Waves splashed against the floats as he lurched upright. This place was his home, too, his dream for the future. He had no intention of letting Logan shut him out and put an end to that dream. He could be every bit as pleasant as she. Cooperative, too. And she'd find out soon enough that nobody worked harder than Mitch Walker.

Just remember . . . stick to business. Forget the romantic stuff.

Right. All he had to do was stop thinking about Logan as a woman and start thinking about her as his partner. Forget all about stolen moments together. No sunrise at the water's edge, no starry northern sky. Forget about the way her green eyes sparkled whenever she laughed. Forget her soft, pale skin, the lingering scent of fresh spring flowers, the gleam of sunshine in her hair. Just ignore it. Shouldn't be too hard.

Right.

He pushed to his feet, grabbed onto the strut beyond the open cargo door, and swung himself out onto the dock. *Dumb move.*

The rickety boards pitched underfoot; cold water flooded his boots. As he lost his grip on the strut and tumbled headfirst into Thembi's frigid water, Mitch swore. And then he laughed. His new partner would probably say he had it coming.

Logan climbed the stairs slowly, her footsteps muffled by the threadbare carpet covering the treads. She'd been too sleepy yesterday to notice it was almost worn through in places. This, she quickly decided, would be her next job. Pull up the old carpet and lay new. Gramps was likely to catch a toe, and if he fell again . . . well, next time he might not be so lucky.

She'd have to repaint, too. New carpet would make the pale green walls look even more faded and out-of-date. And once she painted the stairwell and hall, she'd have to do the living room and bedrooms. She was beginning to understand why this place was in such rough shape. Every job, no matter how small, turned up a half dozen more things in need of attention.

"What we could use around here," she said to herself, "is another pair of helping hands." She wondered how Mitch and Gramps would react when she told them she knew exactly where to find their willing helper.

Mitch might be hard to convince. Given his Neanderthal attitude to "city girls," goodness only knew how he'd react to a teenager who'd never been north of Bloor Street. Gramps, on the other hand . . . He'd always been such a softy where kids were concerned, and so interested in hearing about her "hard cases." She was almost certain he'd see the wisdom in her plan. If not, she'd just have to find a way to convince him.

She paused in the living room doorway to watch him sleep. He was snoring contentedly, sprawled on the sofa with a rumpled newspaper open on his chest and both feet dangling over the edge. She smiled fondly, remembering all the stories he'd told her about how Grammy used to get "hoppin' mad" whenever she caught him with his shoes on the furniture.

Grammy had passed away the year before Logan was born, but the old man still thought of her each and every day, and he still respected her wishes. *Talk about true love.* She'd grown up believing there'd be someone in her future, someone who'd love her the way Gramps loved Grammy. Her years in the city had put a few dents in the dream, but part of her still clung to the hope of one true, forever love—husband, friend, partner.

Partner. She tried to imagine what a man like Mitch Walker would think of her romantic notions of love and devotion, then had to cover her mouth with both hands to hold back the laughter. Just as well he'd never find out. From now on, she'd stick to business with Mr. Walker. It was the only way to win his trust, to convince him she was partnership material and, along the way, unlock whatever secrets he was keeping.

Across the room, Gramps stirred restlessly in his sleep. Logan moved silently through the door, stopping to pick up the newspapers strewn on the floor. A couple of weeks' worth . . . but none of them *this* week. She glanced at the date on the issue draped across Casey's chest—*May?* With a shock, she realized how thoroughly city life had spoiled her. News, and anything else she could think of, was ready and waiting twenty-four hours a day, every day. Here in the north, things were a whole lot different. The newspaper came by mail, and the mail waited in Indigo Bay until someone had time to fly out and pick it up. Current news, of course, was available on the radio. But obviously, just like when she was a little girl, Gramps still loved to browse his newspapers. She remembered how he used to look forward to getting a stack of them with his mail, and then he'd set them aside and read them in order, one day at a time.

She stacked the papers, placing them carefully on the end table in case Gramps hadn't finished reading them. It felt so strange to be tidying this room again, almost as if she'd stepped back in time. The windows, overlooking the guest cabins and lake, were draped with the same heavy, rose-patterned curtains she remembered from her childhood. Good for keeping out the drafty winter chills, Gramps always said. And roses were Grammy's favorites. Behind the curtains, a set of wide-slatted, wooden Venetian blinds blocked the afternoon sun, casting a pattern of light and dark stripes across the faded oriental rug.

Lovingly, Logan straightened the antimacassar on the back of the old wing chair. When she was little, its delicate pattern of butterflies and lace had so fascinated her, she'd begged Ruby to teach her how to crochet. Goodness knows the poor woman had tried, but her tomboy student had been all thumbs. She grinned. Give Logan Paris an Evinrude in need of a tune-up and she'd have it purring by dinnertime. But when it came to the gentler arts, things like knitting, sewing, and darning socks . . . well, as far as she was concerned, ''darn'' was something you said right before you dumped a holey sock into the trash can.

She sank onto the chair, kicking off her deck shoes and tucking her legs up underneath her. With almost reverent care, she chose a familiar photo from the collection of framed snapshots on the coffee table. A young couple smiled up at her from beneath the glass, a woman with auburn hair and laughing green eyes, arm-in-arm with a dark-haired, handsome man. Her parents. Smiling wistfully back at them, Logan tried to recall the sound of their voices, their laughter, the touch of their hands. But it was so long ago and her memory of them had faded until she couldn't see their faces without a picture.

''Fine-lookin' couple, they were.'' Casey grabbed onto the back of the couch and pulled himself up, grumbling about stiff old bones as he yawned, stretched, and reached for his cane. ''So, how'd the berry pickin' go?''

''Fine.''

Casey leaned forward, raising a bushy eyebrow as he met her gaze. *''Fine?''*

Logan struggled to keep a straight face as she returned the precious photo to its place of honor. Apparently, when it came to being evasive, Gramps could dish it out but he didn't much like taking it.

"Ruby's probably got the pies in the oven by now. We filled all four baskets . . . would've had more if we hadn't eaten so many along the way."

"Never could resist 'em myself," said Casey with a wink. "What about you an' young Mitch? Did you get around to talkin' 'bout bein' partners?"

"No, not exactly."

"Eh? What's that mean, 'not exactly'?"

"Well, I tried, but . . . I don't think he's too happy about it, Gramps."

"That so?" Casey folded his arms across his chest and studied her with a thoughtful frown.

Logan endured the silence as long as she could. "How come you never told Mitch about me?"

His eyebrow arched again. "I didn't?"

"He thought your granddaughter was still a little kid."

"Little kid, eh? Huh! What d'you know 'bout that?"

"Sounds to me as if you two don't really know each other all that well. How'd you ever get to be partners?"

"Now, Lily, he's the quiet type, is all. Keeps pretty much to himself, y'know? Always had the feelin' he had things he'd just love to talk about, but didn't quite know how. So, we always wound up talkin' business." He chuckled. "I suppose I might have told him a few Lily stories, but . . ."

"*Lily stories?* Oh, boy!"

Judging from the sly grin the old man was wearing, he'd probably told all the really embarrassing ones . . . like the time she ran out the back door, straight into a passing skunk. Guests had avoided her for at least a week, even after three soaks in tomato juice. Or maybe he'd revealed the awful truth about the time she "helped" Ruby make apple pies. Everybody said they were the finest-looking pies they'd ever seen. Trouble was, the crust was so tough it would've taken a chainsaw to hack off a slice.

Oh well, if they were going to be partners, Mitch would find out soon enough that she didn't have a domestic bone in her body. She had lots of other useful talents, though. Used to be the best fishing guide Casey Lodge ever had, next to Gramps and Andy Twelvetrees, of course. She'd had a knack for finding the big lakers. And Walt Logan always said she was a natural when it came to flying. If Auntie Pearl hadn't insisted on taking her to Toronto on her fifteenth birthday, she'd have had her pilot's license by the end of that summer. Maybe Mitch would let her practice. . . .

Hah! Let a city girl fly his Old Beauty? That'd be the day! Although it might be kind of fun to ask, if only to see his reaction.

"Gramps? Yesterday, you said something about papers Mitch wants you to sign. What's that all about?"

"Ach! The boy's got it into his head that this D'Or-On bunch is gonna steal the place right out from under us."

"What?"

"Pfffft! Nonsense, is all. Thembi's been in O'Malley hands since my grandpappy's day. He used to run trap lines back in the bush, did I tell you 'bout that?"

Logan nodded. She'd grown up on O'Malley stories, tales of trappers and loggers, and the joys and hardships those early northern pioneers had faced. Always O'Malley land. But now . . . What if Mitch was right?

"He must have good reason to be worried, Gramps. Shouldn't we at least—"

"Now, you listen up, little girl. I'll tell you same as I told the boy. Ain't *nobody* got a claim on this land or Casey Lodge 'cept Casey." Thumping his cane on the floor for emphasis, he added, "And you can take *that* to the bank!"

"But, Gramps . . ."

"Don't worry yourself, little girl." Casey held up his hand, one gnarled finger pointing in her direction, his meaning perfectly clear. Subject closed.

"Stubborn" was the word most often used when it came to describing Casey O'Malley, and once he'd pointed that finger of his, there was no use arguing. Like it or not, Mitch was going to have to give up the silent partner act and talk to her about D'Or-On. The whole situation was giving her a very bad feeling.

Casey pushed stiffly to his feet. "Best get back to my plumbin', I suppose."

"Hmm. Something else you haven't told me about."

"Eh?"

"Ruby says you're working on a new cabin."

"She told you that, did she?"

"Mmm-hmm."

"Well, no big secret, little girl." He was smiling, eyes twinkling with the same cryptic humor she'd seen on Ruby's face. What was so special about this new cabin? Come to think of it, why was he working on a new one at all when the other six were so badly in need of repair? She caught herself frowning over the puzzle and forced herself to return his smile.

"So, can I help? I'm pretty good with a pipe wrench, y'know. And we could talk some more . . ."

"Lily, Lily, I do believe you're thinkin' too hard again. And you're lookin' tired, too. I know you're eager to get to work, bein' a partner an' all. But you oughta have yourself a bit of a holiday first. Relax!"

"I don't want to relax, Gramps. I want this place to shine again, and there's so much to do!"

"There is at that. C'mere, little girl." With a chuckle, Casey pulled her into his arms, dropping a gentle kiss on the top of her head, hugging her the way he used to whenever she was worried or upset.

Logan hugged him back, resting her cheek on his shoulder,

relishing the welcome-home feeling of her grandfather's embrace. His shirt smelled like the outdoors, piney and fresh, and even though he didn't seem quite as big as he used to, she sensed he was still strong and capable. She could feel the work-hardened muscles in his arms.

It would be so easy to believe he was right, that no one and nothing could hurt him or threaten their home, their future. But Mitch's words still haunted her. . . .

"If somebody wanted to, it'd be pretty easy to take advantage of Casey."

Chapter Nine

*G*ood job. No, better than good. Logan had the old chair looking almost new again. Mitch ran his hand over the armrest and smiled his approval. Not a single rough spot remained. Not a speck of that ugly green paint, either. The scraping and sanding must have taken her hours to finish. No wonder she'd flaked out.

He inched closer, shoving both hands into his pockets—the only way to be certain he wouldn't give in to temptation. Logan was sitting sideways in another of the rustic old chairs, knees tucked up in front of her, paint scraper still in hand. She'd wrapped her arms around her legs and fallen sound asleep, head resting comfortably on her grass-stained knees.

His ''temptation'' was a wispy strand of auburn hair, an escapee from her neatly tied ponytail. Teased by the light summer breeze, it danced across her cheek, tickled her nose, and played on her lips. *Lucky wisp.*

If he brushed it away, would she wake and find him watching? Would she reward him with a warm, sleepy smile? He tried to imagine her reaction, then thought of how shamefully he'd treated her a few hours ago, and quickly decided to keep his hands to himself.

Hadn't he vowed to forget about all this touchy-feely stuff and get on with business? He shouldn't even be *thinking* about her hair, much less imagining how it would feel, slipping soft and silken between his fingers.

But still he watched, memorizing the way she wrinkled her nose, the steady, gentle rhythm of her breath, every soft, contented sound she made in her sleep.

Asking for trouble.

He took a single step back, not quite ready to turn away. A quiet moment like this one might never come again. He was still hesitating when Ruby rang the dinner bell. Not really a bell at all, but an enormous forged triangle. According to Ruby, it had been hanging outside the kitchen window for as long as anyone could remember. Struck with a metal rod, it announced meal times in a voice that echoed cheerfully down the lake and through the woods. Cheerful and, at this close range, painfully loud.

Logan practically flew out of her chair, gasping in wide-eyed confusion. ''What? I . . .'' She stumbled, reaching out to him as if to steady herself.

''It's all right, I've got you.'' *Don't do it!* Too late. His arms had already closed around her. And Logan wasn't resisting.

Say something! ''Uh . . . dinner bell. I was just coming to wake you. Hungry?''

''Uhn.'' Her head nodded onto his shoulder. ''Must've fallen asleep. Bus lag's catching up to me, I guess.''

''Bus lag?''

She groaned again. ''Yeah. Like jet lag. Only worse.''

''Rough trip, huh?'' Mitch closed his eyes, let his chin rest lightly on the top of Logan's head, and lifted his hand to smooth her hair. How could this possibly be wrong? She felt so right in his arms.

Different woman, different place . . . same deep trouble. It felt right the last time, too, remember?

He remembered. Five years ago, back when he still believed in love.

''Yeah, rough,'' she said softly, her voice still heavy with sleep. ''Thirty-three hours of rough. The old couple in the seats behind mine must've lost their hearing aids. They spent most of the trip hollering at each other.''

She yawned then, her hands moving hesitantly against his chest. Did the embrace feel right to her, too, or was she finally waking up, getting ready to push him away?

Just like before.

But it wasn't like before. Five years ago, he'd let himself fall for another woman. Smart and pretty, with hair the color of midnight and eyes so full of promises—a city girl who'd thought their life in the north would be one long day at the beach. She hadn't counted on blackflies or bears in the backyard or snowdrifts that could swallow up a house. Logan was different. Logan had grown up here.

She sighed. ''I *hate* buses.''

Maybe not so different, after all. She'd been away for ten years, remembering all the good times and forgetting about the bad. She might think this was what she wanted, but living here after a decade of comfort and convenience was a whole other story. And a whole lot rougher than a bus ride.

''Well, well, well . . . what's this?''

''Gramps!''

Logan pulled free. Mitch watched a blush rise hotly on her cheeks as she turned to face Casey.

''I . . . that is . . . the bell. I was asleep. We sort of . . . we had a collision.''

''So I see,'' said Casey.

His exaggerated wink drew an irate scowl from Logan. ''I'll see you at dinner,'' was all she said before she turned and stomped into the house.

Casey chuckled. ''That girl never did like bein' proved wrong.''

''Wrong? About what?''

''Eh?'' Casey frowned. ''I suppose now you're gonna tell me I didn't just catch you with your arms around each other.''

"Well, yeah, but . . ."

"Looked to me as if you're doin' a pretty good job of workin' out your differences, eh?"

Mitch shrugged. *Not even close.* But the old man didn't need to hear the sorry truth. It would only upset him to know his two partners hadn't been able to finish a single conversation.

"You're not worried 'bout workin' with Lily, are you, boy? 'Cause I want you to know that it don't change things between us. Not one bit. Only that we'll have to start includin' her." He slapped Mitch soundly on the shoulder. "You two'll make fine partners, just wait an' see. And y'never know," he added, as a sly grin crept across his face, "maybe you'll decide on another kind of partnership, too."

Casey walked away, leaning heavily on his cane and chuckling to himself, obviously not expecting any sort of a response. Good thing. Because for the second time today, Mitch was speechless.

"Merciful goodness, child, what's wrong?"

"Wrong? N-nothing. Nothing's wrong."

Avoiding Ruby's scrutiny, Logan slouched into the corner and turned her baleful gaze on the kitchen door. She should've gone straight to her room but instead she'd stormed through the dining room and into the kitchen and now the stupid door was rocking back and forth on its big swing hinges like . . . like . . . *Exactly* like her emotions when it came to Mitch Walker.

Wishing she'd had a proper door to slam, she pushed away from the wall, drew a deep, steadying breath, and forced herself to look up at Ruby. The woman wasn't buying her "nothing's wrong" line, but at least she'd gone back to stirring her soup instead of staring.

"I must have fallen asleep out front. The dinner bell startled me. That's all."

"I see. Strange, isn't it?"

Logan crossed the room to lean on the counter, resting her chin in her hands as she watched Ruby stir the fragrant concoction of vegetables, meat, and broth. "What's strange?"

"Well, after all those years in Toronto, I'd have thought you'd be used to loud noises. You never were the nervous type."

"Don't tease."

"No? Well, then, don't be tellin' me half-truths. What's goin' on?"

"I don't . . . that is . . ."

Her breath shuddered out on a sigh, loud and long and utterly pitiful-sounding. What on earth was the matter with her? Apparently Ruby was wondering the same thing. The old wooden spoon hovered halfway between the pot and her lips.

"I'm not exactly sure what's going on."

"I see."

Ruby tasted the soup, nodded her approval, then turned back to Logan and smiled. It was one of those "I know you better than you know yourself" smiles, as much a part of life at the Lodge as lake trout for breakfast on Sunday mornings. There'd been many times when Logan had found that smile impossibly annoying, but as she'd grown older she'd had to admit, Ruby was usually right.

"Why don't you wash up?" said Ruby, still wearing her know-it-all grin as she dropped the wooden spoon into the sink. "You can take the bread and salad out to the table for me, too. Maybe by then you'll have figured it out."

"Sure." Smiling in spite of herself, Logan moved to the sink, pausing to give the older woman a quick kiss on the cheek before she turned on the tap.

"Ruby?"

"Hmm?"

"Did you ever do something you really didn't mean to, something you probably shouldn't have, but then when you did it felt kind of . . . right?''

''Of course, child. 'Most everyone has, I suppose.''

'' *'Most everyone.'* '' The thought was pleasantly reassuring. Logan lathered and rinsed, then gave the tap a twist. Of course, '' 'most everyone'' wasn't dealing with Mitch Walker, the most chauvinistic, incommunicative, irritating, sympathetic, tender, unpretentious . . . in short, the most confusing man in the known universe. And if Gramps hadn't interrupted when he had . . .

Logan leaned heavily against the sink and let her eyes fall shut for a brief moment. She could still feel the warmth of Mitch against her, the gentle strength of his embrace, the way his powerful hands moved so lovingly through her hair.

No! He was destined to be her business partner, nothing more. But until she could satisfy herself that his intentions really were honorable, she couldn't afford to think of him as anything more than a player in the game. And it was up to her to get the upper hand. She yanked a towel off the rack and rubbed her hands dry. Too bad she couldn't wipe away the memory of his touch so easily.

''Did something you shouldn't have, eh?'' said Ruby sagely. ''Child, something tells me you're not talkin' about eatin' a whole box of chocolates by yourself.''

Logan shrugged. ''No, not exactly.''

Ruby caught her by the arm, stopping her as she reached for the salad bowl.

''We'll talk about it later, okay, Ruby?''

The older woman made a sour face. ''Might want to clean up those knees a bit, too,'' she said, shaking her head as she pointed at Logan's legs. ''I declare I was tellin' you the same thing before dinner ten years ago.''

Logan looked down at her grass-stained knees and groaned. Ruby was right. She looked more like a troublesome little kid—

and a tomboy at that—than a full-grown, capable woman. Had Mitch noticed? Did it matter?

Telling herself it *didn't* matter, not in the least, she grabbed a handful of paper towels, wet them under the tap, and started scrubbing. After all, she'd earned this grime doing good, honest work. Work that would benefit all of them in the long run. Mitch was likely to see her in much worse states than this as the summer wore on. And it simply *didn't* matter.

She scrubbed a bit harder.

If it didn't matter, why did she suddenly feel so embarrassed? And worse, why couldn't she stop thinking about him?

It had seemed so natural to lean on his shoulder, so comforting to feel his arms around her, and yet so utterly surprising just a moment later. And she wasn't the only one who'd been caught off guard. No, if she had to give a name to the expression she'd seen on Mitch's face after Gramps interrupted them, surprise would be right at the top of her list.

"That's enough, dear." Ruby's hand settled firmly on her shoulder. "I think they're sterile now. Clean enough to eat off of."

With one more swipe for good measure, Logan tossed the soiled paper into the trash. "You're teasing again."

"And you're off in the clouds, daydreamin'."

"Sorry, Ruby. I'm just a little preoccupied."

"Oh? Hadn't noticed." She chuckled. "I've been a bit that way myself this afternoon."

"Oh? Why's that?"

"Your granddaddy got hold of Andy for me on that radio of his. Kinda hard to hear, what with the static an' all, but the important thing is, Andy's safe. And they're finally gettin' the fire under control."

"Oh, thank goodness!" Catching Ruby in a quick hug, Logan added, "You must be so relieved." She felt a rush of relief herself, even though she hadn't been consciously worrying about the distant fire. "Will he be coming home soon?"

"Child, this hasn't been home for him since the year after you went away. Not in fire season, anyway."

"Oh, right. Gramps wrote me about his, um, 'adventures.' "

"Adventures? More like he's . . ." Ruby hesitated, catching her lower lip in her teeth as deep furrows creased her brow.

"What? Ruby, don't shut me out, please."

"I'm not tryin' to shut you out, dear. Just don't want to upset you, is all."

"Upset? What do you mean? Why would hearing about Andy upset me?"

"Because, child. Because of what he does."

"Fire." Logan's tongue seemed to stumble over the word. She wrapped her arms around herself and studied the red linoleum on the kitchen floor. There'd been times, when she was very little, when she'd been afraid to walk on it, certain she could see flames dancing across its polished surface.

"You were too young to remember," said Ruby, her voice wavering, "but Andy . . . You're as close to a baby sister as he'll ever have, you know?"

"I know."

Logan traced a line across the floor with the toe of her shoe. *Too young to remember.* Too young? Or too afraid?

"He suffered right along with you when you were growin' up, havin' those nightmares you used to get . . ."

"Still get," murmured Logan, forcing herself to meet Ruby's gaze. "Gramps wouldn't talk about it with me. Or maybe he couldn't, I don't know. But now . . . Ruby, I *need* to remember. Will you help me?"

"Of course, child. Any way I can. Andy would be the one, though. He was with your granddaddy when . . ."

Eyes glistening with unshed tears, Ruby turned away. Wiping her hands on her apron, rummaging in the drawer for a ladle, pulling four bowls off the shelf, she used her busyness like a shield. Finally, as she concentrated on filling the first bowl with soup, she continued.

"Now it's like the boy's on a mission, you know? Like he's got to prove he can beat the fire." Her plump hands trembled, splashing soup onto the counter instead of into the bowls. Ruby ignored it.

"We were hoping he'd be back for a bit . . . your granddaddy and Mitch could sure use the help. But Andy says there's another fire burning to the south and if they don't need him there, like as not they'll send him off to Manitoba."

Logan slipped her arm around Ruby's waist and held tight, resting her head on the woman's broad back. All these years she'd let herself believe the dark memories and terrifying dreams had only affected her. That she alone had been too weak or too afraid to deal with the past. But Andy's crusade and Ruby's quiet anguish proved her wrong. She wasn't alone.

"Uh, 'scuse me."

Mitch's voice from the doorway brought Logan to attention. He looked embarrassed, she thought. And concerned. Even from halfway across the room, she could feel it, see it in the clear blue eyes that watched her so intently. How much had he heard?

Abruptly, his gaze shifted to Ruby. "Casey's starting to grumble about his dinner, so I said I'd come give you a hand."

Ruby gave a quiet sniff and pasted on a smile. "Almost ready. Why don't you help Logan with the salad and bread?"

"Okay."

He smiled awkwardly, almost nervously, as he approached the counter and accepted the bowl of salad from Logan . . . as if he thought it might be dangerous to get too close to her.

Remembering how tenderly he'd held her, the gentle touch of his hand in her hair, and the surprising warmth his embrace had sparked, she struggled to contain a smile. Dangerous? If that's what he was thinking, the man just might be right.

Chapter Ten

"One of your hard cases?" Casey's eyebrows twitched. "I dunno, Lily, I'm thinkin' we might be more sorry than glad. Bein' shorthanded is one thing, but tryin' to fix it with a green kid from the city . . . who's gonna look out for him?"

The old man picked up his fork and used it to push the salad around his plate. "*Big* responsibility."

True enough. But it was a responsibility she'd managed quite capably for the last few years, and under much more difficult circumstances.

"You don't know this kid, Gramps. He can look out for himself . . . and has done, for most of his life."

Casey didn't answer, just poked at his salad and gave his head a dubious shake.

It wasn't easy to hide her disappointment. Gramps had always been interested in her students, especially the ones he called her "hard cases." His swift and pessimistic reaction had taken her by surprise.

Maybe she shouldn't have been in such a hurry to bring it up, but Ruby had given her the perfect opener, mentioning once again that Andy wouldn't be coming home. Then, almost as if she knew Logan had the answer, she'd added, "How'll we ever get everything done without him?"

Now, from across the table, Ruby acknowledged her suggestion with a quiet, encouraging nod. She acknowledged Casey's reaction, too—with a sharp nudge of her elbow. The old man just scowled and went back to pushing his salad around, muttering something about rabbit food and how it wasn't meant for humans.

Logan suppressed a smile. Beside her, so close she could feel the warmth of his arm, Mitch buttered a thick slice of fresh bread and said absolutely nothing. Thank goodness for small favors. One negative word from him right now could put an end to her dream before it even got started. Two votes to one.

"There's so much to do this summer, Gramps. And without Andy . . ." She waited through a painfully long silence, then added, "I know this kid. He's willing. He's able. All he needs is an opportunity to prove it. That and a little guidance."

Casey frowned, stabbing at a wedge of tomato on his plate. He didn't look up. "What d'you think, boy?"

Oh, no. The breath she'd been holding slid out in a long, silent sigh. Mitch had made it abundantly clear he considered his new partner a citified liability. And now she wanted to saddle him with more of the same. He wasn't likely to have anything good to say.

"What do I think? Well . . ." He paused, staring down at the spoon in his hand as if he expected to find his answer swimming in Ruby's three-bean soup.

Watching from the corner of her eye, Logan waited while he downed the spoonful and mopped his bowl with a crust of bread.

"I think," he said at last, "this is probably the best soup in the known universe. And . . . I think Logan is right."

Casey's fork clattered against his plate. "She is?"

"I am?" Aware her own expression probably mirrored the wide-eyed surprise she'd just witnessed on her grandfather's face, Logan turned to stare at Mitch.

He shrugged. "Somebody took the time to care about me, once. Gave me a chance. It made a real difference. I always figured I'd repay the favor one day. Sounds to me as if this just might work for all of us."

Mitch spoke with quiet intensity, regarding her with an expression that warned he wasn't ready for questions. She sensed there was much left unsaid, things in his past that still caused him great pain, but she stifled the impulse to reach out, to rest her hand on his and offer comfort. *Someday.* Someday they'd trust each other enough . . .

The thought surprised her. When had they crossed the line, become partners instead of opponents? She felt a rush of warmth at the memory of their embrace. *So right . . .*

Draping one arm over the back of her chair, Mitch leaned close. The merest hint of a smile creased his face, as if he'd been remembering, too. Logan forgot to breathe. If Gramps and Ruby hadn't been sitting across the table, she might have assumed he was getting ready to kiss her. And she might have let him.

"Logan?"

Logan. Same old name, but he made it sound new, full of hope and promise. Her answer squeaked out in a breathless whisper. "Yes?"

"Pass the salad, please."

Logan flailed at the covers, emerging to stare up at her bedroom ceiling with a heartfelt groan. Morning. *Finally!*

Dappled shadows played in the corners as the first rays of sunrise filtered through the ancient pines beyond her window. Once upon a time, Gramps would've been rapping on her door right about now, and the two of them would've crept out of the house and down to the lakeshore, hand-in-hand, fishing rods over their shoulders. But apparently Gramps wasn't rising quite so early these days, and she didn't have the heart to go without him.

Oh, who was she kidding? After tossing and turning for most of the night, the only thing likely to get her out of bed in a hurry was a cup of Ruby's famous coffee. Which, come to think of it, was probably responsible for her unaccustomed wakeful-ness. That and last night's dinner conversation with Mitch and Gramps.

The three of them had stayed at the table long after their meal was finished. They'd polished off two pots of strong coffee, come to a few tenuous agreements, and, all in all, made a fine beginning to their new partnership. *No thanks to you!*

She felt her cheeks grow warm again at the thought of her totally addlepated reaction to Mitch and his unexpected support. Blushing and babbling, she'd acted more like one of the kids she hoped to help than a responsible, capable, *sensible* adult. Logan groaned again. For some reason, good sense seemed to fly out the window where Mitch Walker was concerned.

Curling onto her side, she pulled a pillow into her arms and nestled against it. For one fleeting moment she let herself imag-ine it was him, let herself remember a long-ago dream of some-one to hold, someone to share her life. After last night, it didn't seem quite so impossible anymore.

She'd come home convinced the lodge was her hope for the future, and she'd been equally certain she'd face that future single. After ten years, she'd learned to value her independence, telling herself she didn't need a man or a marriage to make her life complete. She had her kids and Gramps and the lodge. Now she had a new partner, too. And her dream had returned. Was it fate? Had she traveled a long, lonely circle, only to find the thing she wanted most waiting right back where she'd started?

A gentle breeze ruffled the curtains, cooling her face, putting an end to her romantic woolgathering. She had too much work ahead of her to let the morning waste away in daydreams.

Throwing off the blankets, Logan rolled out of bed, gave a long, lazy stretch, and padded across the bare pine floor to lean on the windowsill. A dew-dampened spider's web glimmered jewel-like just beyond the screen and sleepy birds twittered in the branches overhead. They fell suddenly silent as an eerily hollow *thunk* echoed around the lake.

From her east-facing window, Logan couldn't see the shore, but she'd know that sound anywhere—someone had slipped an oar into its lock on one of the old rowboats. Was Gramps up early after all?

Grabbing a blanket to cover the baggy T-shirt she'd worn to bed, Logan dashed out the door and down the hall to the living room. Through the half-open slats of the Venetian blinds, she stared down at the lake and frowned. The early riser wasn't Gramps after all, but Mitch. And whatever he was up to, it *wasn't* fishing. Instead of a rod and reel, he was carrying an axe and, slung over his shoulder, a heavy-looking yellow backpack.

She watched him lug his burden from the boathouse to the shore and settle it into the bottom of the rowboat. He shoved off with one foot, then positioned himself on the center seat and took up the oars. His long, even strokes looked almost as effortless as they were silent and the old boat was soon skimming swiftly across the surface of the mist-shrouded lake.

Her frown deepened. Where was he going? What was he carrying in that bright yellow backpack? More important, why was he sneaking around at the crack of dawn?

She watched for a moment longer, then hustled back to her room to throw on some clothes. It was a glorious morning. The perfect sort of morning to put her old cedar strip canoe in the water and enjoy a before-breakfast paddle. It would be nothing more than coincidence if she happened to encounter her new partner out on the lake.

Mitch rocked back on his heels, tugged the tail of his T-shirt out of his jeans, and used it to mop his brow. He'd left the rowboat tied to a tree nearly an hour ago and had been walking steadily ever since, off the shoreline trail and into the deep forest beyond the raspberry meadow. Every thirty paces, he'd stopped to take a compass reading, then used the axe to blaze a tree, attaching a numbered plastic tag. At the last couple of stations, he hadn't found a tree in the right position and he'd had to trim a sturdy branch to hold the tag, then build a cairn of rocks to keep it upright and secure. It was hot work and he was glad of a moment's rest.

He reached for the backpack, pulled a canteen from the side pocket, and took a long swallow of water. The forest was quiet. Too quiet. For the last fifteen minutes or so, he'd felt strangely unsettled, as if he was being followed. Whatever it was had kept its distance so far, curious but wary. A wolf?

Keeping his movements cautiously slow, Mitch drew the back of his hand across his mouth, then twisted the top back onto the canteen and stowed it away. Behind him, in the distance, another branch crackled. Not a wolf. A porcupine, maybe, or . . . a bear?

Still crouching, he turned to scan the forest. Something rustled, off to the right. A flicker of pale pink in the trees stopped him cold. No bear or porcupine ever wore that color. *Logan.*

He pushed to his feet, deliberately turning his back on the approaching pink shirt, moving slowly away, compass in one hand, axe in the other. She must have awakened early and seen him leave. Or had she stayed awake most of the night the way he had, thinking about her for hours on end, remembering how it had felt to hold her in his arms?

Dream on! She'd been following, watching. She must have seen the tags by now, and if she'd figured out what they meant . . .

The next crackle of branch sounded closer, followed by a brief scuffle in the bushes. Mitch imagined her taking cover behind a tree, holding her breath, hoping he hadn't heard. Good. Now maybe she'd stay put for a minute or two. That was all the time he'd need.

* * *

Logan glared at the broken branch and cursed herself again for being so clumsy. In the old days she'd been able to move through these woods as silently as the shadow that kept her company. This morning, though, it sounded as if she *and* her shadow were wearing clodhopping, branch-snapping army boots.

Swatting angrily at the swarm of mosquitoes buzzing around her head, she finally had to admit Mitch was right about one thing—life in the city had made her soft. She swatted again. Soft and stupid! She should've remembered to slap on some repellent. This deep in the forest, there wasn't enough of a breeze to keep the bloodthirsty little demons at bay.

Logan peered hesitantly around the tree. No sign of Mitch, but his yellow backpack was still on the ground, about fifty feet away. He probably had a nice big bottle of Deet tucked inside. . . .

"Looking for something?"

She spun to face him, flattening herself against the tree trunk, meeting his glare with what she hoped was an equally irate expression. Why on earth had she kept on following him? She already had her proof—an orange plastic tag engraved with a number and the words *Issued by MNDM*. Anyone who'd grown up in the north knew what those initials meant—Ministry of Northern Development and Mines. Mitch was claim-staking. Her gaze shifted to the axe in his hand, the fist clenched in anger. How far would he go to keep his secret?

"What would you have done if I was a bear?"

"A b-bear?" Her mouth felt cottony dry, but it had nothing to do with bears. She'd almost rather face a beast in the woods than deal with Mitch's betrayal. How could he do this to Gramps . . . to her?

"Logan, I'm not a bear and I'm not going to hurt you."

Too late. You already did. She clenched her fists, determined to still the trembling, but anger and adrenaline weren't so easily stilled. What would he do if she had the nerve to say it aloud, to actually tell him he'd hurt her? Would he even care? Raising her chin, she tried to look brave.

He studied her, eyes narrow and piercing. "You were following me. Why?"

"No! I w-wasn't following . . ."

He frowned, shook his head, making her all the more determined to convince him, to buy herself some time to take the evidence back to Gramps.

"No, really. It's such a beautiful morning." That much, at least, was true. "I decided to take the canoe out and . . . and when I saw the boat at the shore, I thought, that is . . . I . . . I . . . Hey! What're you doing?"

Mitch had grabbed her by the hand and was tramping through the underbrush, his long-legged strides forcing her to run to keep up. He growled an answer without turning around, something that sounded to Logan like "take care."

Take care of what? Surely he didn't intend . . .

She tried to pull free but Mitch held tight and hauled her along behind him.

"You were saying?" He released her hand as soon as they reached the clearing where he'd left his backpack. Kneeling to rummage in the pockets, he added, "Something about how you weren't really following me?"

Logan paced, swatting mosquitoes, scratching the bites that now dotted her arms and neck. "I was saying I saw the boat. And then . . ."

Instinctively she backed away from Mitch as he pushed to his feet and moved slowly toward her. "And then I took a walk, and I saw you, and I saw . . . What are you doing?"

"Isn't it obvious?"

A hot blush colored her cheeks as he squirted Deet from a bottle and began slathering it onto her arm. Obvious, indeed. So this was what he meant by "take care."

"Stand still," he said gruffly, spreading the pungent liquid under the sleeve of her T-shirt. It felt cool and soothing against her skin and, despite the gruff voice and grim expression, his touch was gentle, so tender it stole her breath away.

She should tell him to stop. She should take the repellent and finish the job herself. She should. But she didn't. Instead, she let him take her other hand, let him rub the lotion from wrist to shoulder, let her thoughts wander where they had no business going . . . but only for a moment.

"Mitch?"

"Hmm?"

"What's this?" Pulling the stolen claim tag from the pocket of her jeans, she thrust it toward him. "What have you done?"

He didn't answer, gently cupping her face between his hands instead. "Go back, Logan." His thumbs moved carefully over her skin, coating her cheeks and the bridge of her nose with the bitter-smelling liquid. "These mosquitoes are going to get worse. I'll explain everything tonight when I get back, I promise."

Go back? Did he honestly think he could send her packing like a little child? "Does my grandfather know you're staking his property?"

"I'm doing it for him, Logan. And for you."

"Answer me. Does he know?"

She felt him wince before he pulled away, as if the question had hit a sore spot. Shoving his hands into his pockets, he stared down at the yellow backpack, probably trying to come up with a good story, a way to keep her from telling Gramps. That would ruin his plans, all right.

"Well? Does he?"

His jaw tightened. "No. And I'm asking you not to tell him."

"*What?* Why on earth would I keep this from him? It's his property, Mitch. Not yours. What gives you the right?"

"Why can't you trust me, Logan? Your grandfather does."

"Yes. He does. But would he still trust you if he knew what you were doing behind his back?"

Mitch scuffed at the ground with the toe of his boot, a frustrated, helpless sort of gesture. "Casey thinks he's got some kind of automatic rights because his family has owned this land forever. Well, he's wrong. But he won't listen to me. And he's made his little 'it's mine and that's that' speech in front of those D'Or-On lackeys enough times. I'm afraid they'll just keep on staking when they get to lodge property and steal the mineral rights out from under us. What'll that do to him, Logan? And how do you think our guests will react when a mine goes in next door?"

"You mean . . . Are you saying they can claim mineral rights, even if they don't own the land?"

"*Exactly.* But once it's staked and registered, we won't have to worry. And Casey doesn't ever have to know, unless you tell him. Look at it as protecting your own interests."

Logan stared at him for a long moment, then began pacing again. If what he'd said was true, his plan made a lot of sense. Oh, how she wanted to believe him, and that was the problem. She wanted it too much. Feelings or not, she'd never be really sure of him until she'd checked out his story for herself.

Mitch stopped her, resting his hands on her shoulders. "Trust me," he whispered, touching her hair and her cheek, looking down at her with the same hopeful, nervous expression she'd seen yesterday after the dinner bell had sent her flying into his arms. It made her want to forget all the doubts and fears and just believe in him. It made her want to lose herself in his arms. But Mitch had other ideas.

"You'd better get back. There's a lot of organizing to do if you're going to bring that kid up for the summer. Best get at it, don't you think?"

"It's already organized—well, mostly. I figured I'd be able to convince Gramps it was a good idea, so I just went ahead and made the arrangements before I left. A friend of mine from school will handle things from that end. All I have to do is let her know when to send him.''

''Well, good. Go do it, then. I sure won't complain about a little help with this job, either.'' He reached for the backpack, swinging it over his shoulder with an exaggerated grunt. ''I'll walk you back to the lake.''

''You don't have to do that.''

''Yes, I do.''

Was he always this stubborn? ''I grew up here, Mitch. I know these woods and I can take care of myself.''

''You can, eh?'' He grinned. Catching her hand in his once more, he ran his fingers over a cluster of already itchy mosquito bites on her wrist. ''Uh-huh. Good job.''

Logan pulled away. ''That's different. It's been a while and I . . . well, I forgot, is all. Doesn't mean I'm going to get lost in the woods or—''

''What about bears? Do you wrestle them by yourself, too?''

''Hey, as long as *you're* whistling, everybody from here to Indigo Bay is safe from bears.''

He scowled. ''Fine. But that tag you pulled off has to go back on its station. So, like it or not, I'm going partway.''

''Honestly, you're so—'' Logan stopped herself. This wasn't about the tag. If he didn't trust her to find the right tree, he could reattach it later on his way back to the boat. No, this was about her, about keeping her safe, and Mitch was wearing a straight-lipped, determined expression that warned she'd be wasting her breath if she argued. Besides, she couldn't deny the effect of his obvious concern. It had been a very long time since anyone had tried to take care of her or protect her. She would've straightened them out pretty quickly if they had. But with Mitch, things were different. It felt so good to know he cared, so right to have him by her side.

''Fine,'' she said at last. ''Partway. But there's a catch.''

"Oh, yeah? What might that be?"

"Tell me about Mitch Walker on the way."

His eyes widened. "About me?"

"Yes, about you—who you are, where you came from." Was it really so hard to believe she'd want to get to know him? "I mean, fair's fair. You've heard a whole raft of Lily stories from Gramps, but when it comes to Mitch stories, it's like you're a mystery man or something. Kind of puts me at a disadvantage, don't you think?"

"I suppose."

Ignoring his dismal frown, Logan turned and started walking back through the forest, marking her path by the next orange tag, barely visible through the brush. "Besides," she added, as Mitch fell into step behind her, "if I can keep you talking, I won't have to listen to that gosh-awful whistle."

Chapter Eleven

"Okay, so . . . exactly what do you want to know?"

Exactly? Logan kept walking, eyes front, shoulders straight, feeling extremely glad Mitch couldn't see the wobbly grin she was wearing.

He reminded her of one of her students, nervous about standing in front of the class to give his report. "Whatever you're comfortable sharing" would've been her stock answer to the student, but in Mitch's case . . . she had a feeling he'd take it as permission to say nothing at all.

"Why not start with where you grew up? Maybe a little about your family? Did you always want to be a pilot?" There. That ought to keep him busy.

She waited. For what seemed like an eternity, the only sound in the forest was the rhythmic tramp of their boots on the pine-littered earth. Simple questions. What could possibly be so difficult about the answers? Unless . . .

Surely he wasn't making something up? Creating the story he thought she wanted to hear?

"Toronto."

One word, but spoken with such raw emotion, Logan could almost believe he'd answered all three of her questions. She glanced back over her shoulder. Head down, Mitch was plodding along behind her, calm on the outside but obviously lost in thoughts of another time and place. Not making it up.

Whether he noticed her scrutiny or not she couldn't tell—he

116

was hiding behind those annoying dark glasses again. "What part of the city?"

"No place you ever visited, that's for sure."

"I wouldn't count on it." Logan sighed, wishing they could stop, find a place to sit, and finish the conversation face-to-face. Bad idea. Mitch was having enough trouble talking to her back. "What I mean is, my school was in a pretty rough neighborhood."

"Oh, yeah? Well, then, let's just say it's not a place I'm eager to see again. Or talk about." He drew a deep breath, as if steeling himself to go on.

"Family . . . There was only me and Mom, but she passed away a long time ago. I never knew my father. Didn't want to. Casey and Ruby are the closest thing to family I've had in a long time."

"Mitch—"

"Don't." His voice crackled with tension. "Just let me say this my way, okay?"

She nodded, fighting the urge to turn and wrap her arms around him, wishing she hadn't started this in the first place. She'd never meant to cause him pain, but the bitterness she was hearing hinted she'd done exactly that.

"My mother worked harder than anyone I've ever known, but it was never enough, you know?"

She knew. She'd heard the story time and again from her students. For some of them, the end of the month meant a choice between eating and paying the rent.

"The summer I turned fifteen, some suit in one of the offices she cleaned offered me a forest service job in a camp north of Thunder Bay."

"Rainbow Country."

"Yeah. It was like a different world, you know? Everything so wild and green and alive. I found out later she'd talked to him about me, told him she was worried I'd get into real trouble if I stayed in the city that summer. She was right. I would've.''

His voice warmed when he talked about his mother and Logan couldn't help feeling she must have been a remarkable woman. Had she lived to see the kind of man her son had become?

''Anyway,'' said Mitch, beginning to sound a little more relaxed, ''that man in the suit took a chance on me, Logan. Probably saved my life. And y'know what? I never even knew his name.''

She smiled. No wonder he was so enthusiastic about her summer kid. This really was his chance to say thank you.

''What's so funny?''

They'd entered a small clearing and Mitch was now walking beside her. She looked up. ''Not funny. But kind of ironic.''

''What is?''

''You said you came north for the first time the summer you turned fifteen.''

''Yeah. So?''

''My Aunt Pearl dragged me off to Toronto on my fifteenth birthday.''

''Dragged? You mean you didn't *want* to go?''

''Well, I was curious, sure. Used to daydream about going south for a visit, just to see what it was like. It all seemed so exotic and exciting. Even so, I'd have done anything in the world to stay here with Gramps. This was home. But he told me to go with Pearl. He told me she was right.''

''Right about what?''

''That my parents would've wanted me to get a good education, make something of my life. So I stayed down south. I did it for them, for Gramps. And I was homesick for ten long years, afraid I'd be letting him down if I packed up and came home.'' She let herself laugh. ''Turns out, Gramps knew all along this was where I belonged. He's just been waiting for me to figure it out.''

Logan looked up to find Mitch grinning at her. ''What?''

He stopped walking, catching her by the elbow to keep her close. ''Just thinking. I'm glad you finally did. Figure it out, that is. Now, where's that claim tag?''

Glad. He was *glad!* She gaped at him for a moment, feeling giddy and strangely off balance, as if her heart was turning cartwheels in her chest. Wrenching her gaze away from his warm smile, she scanned the nearby trees, finally locating the blazed trunk just beyond his left shoulder.

''Good thing you decided to come along,'' she said, fishing the tag out of her pocket. ''I would've missed it.''

''Nah, if I wasn't along, you'd have been paying attention.''

She watched as he fastened the tag into place, marveling at his sudden change of attitude. *A good thing, indeed.* Good for a lot of reasons.

''Over there,'' he said, pointing through the trees. ''You can almost see the lake.''

Logan squinted into the distance. She couldn't see anything but trees.

''Listen.''

He'd moved to stand behind her when she turned her back, and now spoke so softly, so close to her ear, his breath tickled her cheek. It took a long moment, and a lot of willpower, to focus her thoughts outward again.

She listened. Beyond the rustling of branches and the twitter of birds overhead, came the gentle lap-lapping of waves against Thembi's rocky shore.

He spoke again, his tone low and intimate. ''Sure you don't want me to come with you the rest of the way?''

Just the opposite. Logan bit her lip to keep from blurting out the truth. She was sure she *did* want him to come along, if only to spend another ten minutes in his company. There was so much more she wanted to know, so much she longed to share. Not to mention the huge apology owed for following him into the woods the way she had.

She could still feel his breath on her cheek, warm and expectant as he waited for an answer. She didn't dare turn to look at him. Her face felt flushed, her lips dry. If he saw her now, he'd be sure to guess what she was feeling. His apology would have to wait.

"No, I'll be fine . . . really."

"All right, then." He gave her a gentle shove toward the lake. "Better hustle. It's nearly seven. Casey'll be up soon and wondering where the heck you are."

"True."

Worrying Casey and, as a result, drawing attention to Mitch's covert activities in the woods, was the last thing she wanted. He had to be thinking the same thing.

"Why can't you trust me, Logan? Your grandfather does."

She whispered the answer under her breath so Mitch wouldn't hear. *I do trust you.* Why couldn't she say it out loud? Why not turn around, right now, and tell him?

Because she wasn't ready. She wasn't *sure.* Maybe all those years in the city had made her a cynic. Maybe she'd been a science teacher too long. She needed to be more open, trust more freely, take chances with her heart instead of analyzing everything to death. Life didn't always follow scientific method. Mitch's effect on her was proof positive of that. And it was going to take some getting used to!

Forcing herself to put one foot in front of the other, Logan moved slowly away from him. "See you at dinner?"

"Count on it."

Mitch leaned heavily against the nearest tree, jamming both hands into his pockets, scuffling at the earth with the toe of his boot. It had been a long time since he'd shared a glimpse of his past with another person—even Casey didn't know about that first trip north. But Logan was different. It seemed so natural, so right, to share his life with her . . . not easy, but right.

Watching her walk away, he struggled with the urge to follow, to see her safely back to the shore and on her way, but she wasn't likely to appreciate the gesture. *"I can take care of myself."* He could hear it already.

Her pink-shirted figure seemed to hesitate, looking small and alone amidst towering pines and tangled brush, then her voice sang out, "Hey, Walker, you're not whistling!" So confident and self-assured . . . what made him think she needed a protector?

"Yeah, well . . ." He chuckled as she thrashed through a thicket, snapping branches as she passed. "You're not exactly on a stealth mission out there. Don't think either one of us has to worry about bears."

She waved dismissively then vanished over a low rise, leaving Mitch to stare at a wall of green, feeling lonely and strangely ill at ease.

Get back to work. Right. He still had another two miles of perimeter to stake.

Reluctantly hoisting his backpack, he took a couple of steps along the path they'd traveled together, then turned, as if impelled by some unseen force, and followed Logan toward the lake.

He moved slowly, maintaining a cautious distance. She didn't need to know he was keeping an eye on things, but seeing her safely home was the only way he'd could think of to get his mind back where it belonged for the rest of the day—*on his work.* Not that his mind showed any sign of straying from thoughts of Logan. What had she been thinking when she followed him into the woods? What had she expected to find?

Exactly what she did find—evidence. His gut tightened. Sure, she'd made a good show of believing his story, but what if she still had doubts? What would happen to all his plans, his dreams for the future, if she went back to Casey Lodge and shared those doubts with her grandfather? He couldn't let that happen.

Pondering what he'd say to convince her, once and for all, Mitch gradually closed the distance between them, not stopping until he reached the ridge where he'd last seen Logan's pink shirt among the trees. From his vantage point, the land sloped steeply down to Thembi's rugged shore—a rocky bluff, strewn with jagged, moss-covered boulders and the decaying remains of a dozen fallen trees. He could see the old rowboat, bobbing at the end of its tether line, and Logan's canoe, upturned on the rocks nearby, but Logan herself had vanished.

Mitch wasn't prepared for the wave of panic that ripped through him as he struggled to rid himself of the heavy back-pack. He was running before it hit the ground, sliding from rock to rock, handhold to handhold, heart pounding like thunder as he descended the steep slope. Where was she? Had she slipped? Struck her head on a rock? Fallen into the lake? He should have insisted on walking with her. If he had . . .

Please, let her be all right, he prayed silently.

Skidding to a halt at the water's edge, he scanned the shore-line for a glimpse of pink shirt. Nothing.

His breath came in sharp, ragged gasps. He had to force him-self to stand still, to breathe slowly and calmly, to ease the pounding rhythm of his heart . . . to listen.

The forest and lake seemed eerily quiet. Only the faint lap-ping of water, the rustling of a gentle new breeze in the trees. No birdsong. No chatter of squirrels.

''Logan?''

No answer.

Turning, he searched the hillside, seeking a flash of pink among the fallen logs and rocky outcroppings, but Logan was nowhere to be seen. It was as if she'd vanished into thin air.

Think. If she hadn't been injured, where would she go? *Of course!* The meadow where they'd picked raspberries yesterday was only a short hike away. Too bad he hadn't thought of that before he risked his neck for her.

Mitch scrambled back up the bluff, following a diagonal path to the crest of the ridge overlooking the meadow. If he'd guessed right, he'd be able to see her from there.

Thoughts of what he might do to make her pay for giving him such a scare were soon banished by memories of ripe, juicy berries. His dry mouth puckered with anticipation as he realized how thirsty he'd become. *Pretty stupid to leave the canteen behind.* No, stupid had nothing to do with it. When he'd dropped that backpack, Logan's safety had been his only thought.

He forged on, climbing faster, ignoring the burn in his muscles until, at last, he half-threw himself over a boulder and onto the sunny, bald ridge. As soon as he caught his breath, he'd let out a bellow loud enough to frighten every living thing between here and Casey Lodge. See how she—

Below him, bathed in morning dew and twinkling in the sunlight, the meadow stretched lush and green . . . and empty.

"Logan?" Not a bellow, after all, but merely a whisper. Her name caught in his throat. This wasn't possible. People simply didn't vanish.

Pacing to the far side of the rock, Mitch stared down into the sheltered valley below. He could see the lakeshore trail where it wound through the trees in the distance. And, just beyond the meadow, the black, ruined chimney of the cabin Logan had called home.

Half-running, half-sliding, Mitch descended the smooth rock face and bounded across the meadow. It wouldn't be nearly so quick and easy going back—they'd have to find another way around the bald rock. But going back didn't seem to matter to him right now. All that mattered was finding Logan. He wasn't sure why, but he felt certain he knew where she'd gone.

He was right. Wrapping one arm around the smooth, silvery green trunk of a young poplar, Mitch let the sturdy tree support his weight while he caught his breath. Across the clearing, Logan stood with her back to him, motionless and silent, head bowed as if in prayer, auburn hair gleaming in the sunlight. The blackened chimney of the old cabin seemed to tower over her like a specter.

She sank slowly onto the ground as he watched, wrapping her arms around her legs. As her forehead touched her knees, she began to sob.

Her sorrow followed the sound in waves—so real it seemed to fill up the space between them, stilling the crickets and hushing the birds in the trees. It felt to Mitch as if the whole world was holding its breath, waiting for him to do something. Anything. But what right did he have to intrude on her pain, or even to witness her sorrow? No right. But every need.

Unbidden, his feet carried him across the clearing. He *needed* to hold her, *needed* to comfort her, *needed* to know the reason for the sorrow that now enveloped them in its pall. And, whether she knew it or not, Logan needed all those things, too.

"Logan?" He murmured her name as he sank onto the ground behind her, pulling her close, sheltering her in his arms. "What's wrong?"

He measured time by his own heartbeats in the long, empty silence that followed. Twelve, thirteen, fourteen, before she finally whispered an answer.

"I . . . I remember."

"Remember?" He looked up at the fire-blackened chimney, the ruined stone wall. "The fire?"

Logan nodded mutely, leaning into his embrace as if she knew how much he longed to ease her pain. He wanted to kiss the tears from her eyes and help her forget, but he sensed she needed something more. She needed to remember.

Holding her closer, matching each breath to hers, Mitch rested his cheek against the soft, spun silk of her hair. "Tell me."

She trembled, then clenched her fists, as if grabbing a handful of courage. "It . . . it was dark. I could hear . . . I don't know. Nothing I'd ever heard before, or since. Flames, I guess. The roar of the fire. And smoke. I c-couldn't breathe. Like when we were up in the plane and you . . . you wanted w-wet towels."

"Logan, I'm so sorry."

"You didn't know. How could you?" She sniffed, swiping at her tears as another sob wracked her body. "I remember Daddy yelling. And I was afraid until he came to get me. And then I saw the flames. I remember how he ran through the flames with me in his arms. And then he left me in the grass. And I c-couldn't move, because . . . because my blankets were all tight around me. And it w-wasn't dark anymore. The whole sky was red. And Daddy was yelling, calling my mother's name. B-but she—she d-didn't answer. And . . . and . . . and . . ."

"Shh. Take it easy, Logan. You don't have to—"

"*Yes!* Y-yes, I do. I have to remember b-because now . . . now I understand."

"What? What do you understand?"

"The n-nightmares. Mitch, they're never about the flames or about Daddy yelling."

"Then . . . what?"

"They're always about how . . . how *quiet* it was after he stopped."

Mitch held his breath, uncertain of what to do or how to comfort her. No child should have to see what she'd seen, endure the pain, the loss, the nightmares. Small wonder she'd blocked out the memories.

She turned, slipping one arm around him, resting her head on his chest, close to his heart. He wondered what she heard in its racing rhythm. Did she know it was full-to-bursting with tenderness and new emotions? Did she know those new feelings were all for her? Too bad he couldn't find a way to tell her. But he could hold her. And hold her he did.

"Thank you," she said, so softly he barely heard the words.

"For what?"

"For coming after me. For letting me tell you."

Mitch pressed his lips to the top of her head in a gentle kiss. "Hey, that's what partners are for, right?"

Logan looked up at him, face streaked with tears, and somehow managed a crooked smile. "Right. Thanks, partner."

Partner. The word meant more than she could possibly know. The chance to be a part of Casey Lodge, to build the future with his own two hands, was a dream come true. And Logan had just delivered the means to make it happen. "Come on, I'll take you home."

"But what about—"

"It'll wait. We'll get that city kid of yours out into the bush for a day . . . finish the job in half the time."

Logan sniffed, laughing weakly as she swiped her tears away. "Yeah, right. Either that, or we'll never be seen again."

Chapter Twelve

"So . . . tell me some more about this kid you've hired to, um, *help* us. What've Casey and I gotten ourselves into?"

Logan stopped scratching the mosquito bites on her wrist and slowly—*very* slowly—looked up. She was seated, cross-legged, in the stern of the old rowboat, with Mitch's backpack wedged in behind her. It made a lumpy but reasonably comfortable cushion. And Mitch made one heck of an impressive sight.

Bronzed and toned to perfection, muscles straining against his T-shirt with each rhythmic stroke of the oars, he glanced down at her and smiled. "What'd you say his name was?"

"Ryan. Ryan Anders."

Logan settled back against her makeshift pillow, wondering self-consciously if Mitch realized she'd been ogling him again. Good grief, why bother importing a teenager from the city? She was behaving like one herself! Thankfully, the object of her ogling seemed oblivious.

"He just turned sixteen. And I suppose I'd have to say this whole thing was his idea in the first place."

"Oh, yeah?"

Mitch had been staring into space, concentrating on the lift, reach, and pull of rowing, sparing her the occasional glance, but now his gaze fell squarely on her. With sunlight glinting off his dark glasses and a gentle breeze teasing his raven hair, he smiled again, a little silent encouragement for her to get on with the story.

127

"You'll like him, I think. He's a bit of a smart aleck, but it's all show." *A lot like a certain pilot I know.*

Mitch chuckled. "Sounds familiar."

His expression left little doubt he was talking about her, not himself. Logan responded with a whoop of laughter. "I was thinking *exactly* the same thing! *Almost.*"

The oars made a hollow *thunk* as Mitch rested them on the gunwale. He rolled his shoulders and studied her thoughtfully, a wry smile curling his lips. "Smart-alecky? *Me?*"

His eyebrows arched, twitching above the frames of the dark glasses, and Logan whooped again. "Let's just say you and I are two of a kind and leave it at that, okay? Ryan should fit right in. Want me to row for a while?"

"And miss my weekly workout? No thanks." He reached for the oars and dipped them into the water, quickly falling into his rowing rhythm again.

Thank goodness! Hoping her relief wasn't as obvious as it felt, Logan glanced over her shoulder at the cedar strip canoe they were towing. With its tether line fastened securely to the stern of the rowboat, it trailed along in their wake, looking utterly abandoned and forlorn. Strangely enough, she had no wish to keep her trusty old fishing companion company. At least, not now. She'd felt quite proud of the way she'd been able to handle the canoe after so many years away, but while her brain had remembered exactly what to do, it appeared her poor citified muscles had completely forgotten.

She scowled at the little boat, absently rubbing her sore arms. Starting tomorrow, she'd do a couple of short paddles every day—emphasize *short*—until she'd whipped herself into shape.

"Problem?" asked Mitch.

She stopped rubbing and flashed a smile. He really didn't need to know, did he?

"Nope. No problem. Just thinking about Ryan. When I first

told the kids I was leaving, most of them looked at me as if I'd grown a second head. *'Whaddaya wanna go live way up there for?'* But Ryan . . . he wanted to hear all about it. Used to come in after class, supposedly to use the computers, but somehow he'd always end up sitting on the corner of my desk, coaxing stories out of me. Then, one day, he asked if Gramps ever hired any summer help. Took me by surprise, to tell you the truth. But it seemed like an awfully good idea. So, I told him that if he could pass the year without having to go to summer school again, I'd see what I could do.''

''I take it he passed?''

''Sure did!'' Logan grinned at the memory of Ryan's impromptu happy-dance in the corridor the day the summer school posting came out. *"Miz Paris, Miz Paris . . . I'm not on the list!"*

''If I'd been certain how Gramps would react, I would've promised that kid a job right then and there. But I wasn't even sure the old grouch would be glad to have *me* back—he always made such a big deal about my future and my education . . .''

''People oughta say what's on their minds,'' said Mitch, suddenly gruff. ''Save a whole lot of heartache.''

Something about the way he said the word ''heartache'' made it sound almost like a confession. Logan scrutinized him. He was staring into the distance again and seemed intent on rowing, jaw clenched, lips set in a thin, tight line. A confession of what? she wondered.

Leave him alone. Right. It was none of her business.

Wrong! They were partners. Someday, maybe, they'd be more. Just an hour ago, back at the old cabin, she'd bared her soul to him and he'd helped her, simply by being there. *"People oughta say what's on their minds."* Well, he asked for it.

''Mitch?''

''Hmm?''

"Why'd you say that? About saving a lot of heartache, I mean."

The question broke his rhythm. One oar flailed, splashing water and thudding against the bow before he picked up the pace again. He grumbled something under his breath—something Logan felt sure she was glad she hadn't heard. Inexplicably, she found herself offering an apology. "Sorry. It's just . . . well, the way you spoke, it sounded . . . personal."

"Personal. Right. So, you thought you'd pry?"

The words stung. Logan pulled her eyes away from his face, stared down at her hands, at the row of itchy, red welts on her wrist. They weren't half as bothersome as the obvious annoyance in Mitch's voice. "I thought," she said quietly, "you might like to say what you meant."

His groan was quickly followed by the dull thunk of oars settling into the bottom of the boat. Mitch leaned toward her, resting his elbows on his knees. "I asked for that one, didn't I?"

She shrugged, looking up to find him wearing a sad smile.

"I've made my share of mistakes in life, Logan. Some worse than others. But only one that really mattered." He passed a hand across his face, pulling the sunglasses off and dropping them into his pocket.

Logan waited. The boat had come to a full stop, bobbing gently with each wave, oarlocks creaking.

"Sure you want to hear this?"

She didn't stop to wonder about his curiously hopeful expression. If she had, she might have considered the possibility he was hoping she'd say no. But, as far as Logan was concerned, there was only one possible answer. "I'm sure."

"Yeah, I figured you would be." Mitch let his head droop into his hands, raking his fingers through his hair. "Okay. Her name was Alison."

Alison? His big mistake was a woman?

"City girl," he continued, in a hollow-sounding voice. "But—"

He straightened, fingering the sunglasses in his pocket as he met her gaze. No. She wouldn't let him hide again. Reaching out, she caught his hand in hers and held tight. "But what . . . ?"

"But . . . Well, for starters, she was *nothing* like you."

Nothing like me. Was that supposed to be a compliment or the world's biggest insult? *Say what you mean.* "Is that a good thing, or . . . ?"

He flashed a wry smile. "Good for you, I suppose. Not so good for Alison. It was death for our relationship. And I was so crazy about her, I didn't even see it coming. She wasn't ready for the kind of life we live up here. She had no idea. . . . And I *couldn't* go back to Toronto. Not to stay. I tried, but that place . . . It's like poison to me."

Turning his hand palm up, Mitch slowly laced his fingers through hers. "I look at you, the things you do, the way you cope with whatever comes along, and I think . . ." He drew a deep breath, stroking gentle circles across her swollen wrist with a calloused thumb.

"Be sure this is right for you, Logan. We *both* need to be sure, before . . ."

She watched him struggle for a moment, then ended the silence for him. "I *am* sure, Mitch. This is my home, my heritage. It's where I belong." *With you.*

Almost as if he'd been thinking the same thing, Mitch lifted her hand to his lips and tenderly kissed her fingertips.

"I know you think this is what you want, Logan. You've been remembering how life used to be and you've missed it. But things change. *People* change. We both know you won't be really sure until you've lived it for a while and— Uh-oh!"

Mitch dropped her hand, directing her gaze ashore with a nod of his head as he reached for the oars and set the old boat in motion again.

Looking over his shoulder, Logan discovered the reason for his sudden activity. Casey was on the beach. Leaning heavily on his cane, one hand shading his eyes from the bright morning sun, the old man watched their progress across the water. They were too far away to read his expression but, for Logan at least, her grandfather's body language left little to the imagination. *"Well, well, well . . . what have we here?"* She could almost hear him, could almost see the sly grin sprouting on his wrinkled face, the curious arch of his bristly eyebrows.

"Uh-oh, is right." She punctuated the statement with a groan. "Now what?"

Mitch grinned. "Oh, I'm sure you'll think of something."

"Me? Why me?"

"Hey, I'm rowing. And anyway, you're the one who decided to turn my quiet morning into a spectator sport." He winked, quashing her objection with a perfectly charming smile.

Logan shrugged. The man was absolutely right. "A picnic! Breakfast meeting out on the lake to talk about our new employee."

"No way! You're dealing with a starving man, here. First thing I want when we hit shore is a big plate of Ruby's pancakes. Maybe some bacon and eggs, too."

"Mmm." Come to think of it, she was pretty darned hungry herself. "Right. Well, maybe—"

"Ahoy, there! Up an' about kinda early this fine mornin', eh? So? What's doin'?"

Casey's voice held a hint of the twinkle Logan knew she would've seen in his eyes, had they been closer. He probably thought they'd been off on some romantic tryst or . . .

She felt a blush warm her cheeks. The way things had worked out, that wasn't too far from the truth. But acknowledging her budding romance with Mitch was one thing; confessing it to

Gramps was a whole other story. She waved at the old man and smiled, steeling herself for the teasing she felt certain they'd have to endure. " 'Morning, Gramps!''

"Don't beach us, Mitch. Slip into the boathouse instead." She glanced up at him, adding, "Less to explain if he doesn't see your backpack."

Nodding, Mitch pulled hard on the port oar, smoothly shifting their course from beach to boathouse. "Good plan. So, what's our story?"

"I wish I knew." She had no intention of lying to Gramps, but she didn't have to tell him the whole truth, either. Mitch would just have to follow her lead, agree with whatever she said. Logan smiled in spite of herself. The prospect didn't sound half bad. "Follow my lead. I'll do the talking and you just nod a lot, okay?"

He chuckled. "Yes, dear."

"Very funny!" She flashed him a sour look, then managed a cheerful smile for her grandfather as they slipped past him and into the boathouse.

Logan hopped out onto the deck with a whispered warning, "Behave yourself. Just remember, we keep your secret, and Gramps won't get upset. It's as simple as that."

"I see. Well, in that case . . ." He grinned wickedly. "Yes, dear."

"Now, cut that out! I *might* get to like it, and *then* what would you do?"

Mitch's grin turned to slack-jawed surprise as she turned away and Logan struggled to contain a smile, satisfied to know her response had caught him off guard. She made a beeline for the door, leaving him to tether the rowboat and lift her canoe out of the water—once he managed to stop sputtering. She ran into Casey just beyond the doorway.

"Whoa, little girl! What's your hurry?"

"We're hungry." Logan slipped her arms around his neck

and gave him a kiss on the cheek, deftly turning him back toward the lodge. "Didn't manage to catch our breakfast, though, so I hope Ruby's cooking up something good."

"Y'been fishin?" Casey quirked one eyebrow and studied her skeptically.

"You might say that," said Mitch, catching up to them as they moved toward the lodge. "Nothin' biting except mosquitoes, though. And your Lily caught our limit of those."

Logan nudged him sharply with her elbow. "Truth is, I decided to take the old cedar strip out for a sunrise paddle and . . . well, I sort of overestimated my stamina." She flexed her arms and made a face. "Mitch to the rescue. Seems like I need a little paddling practice before I try *that* again."

"Yep," said Mitch, moving cautiously out of her reach, "there she was, drifting helpless in the middle of the lake—"

"Helpless? I was not helpless! I—" She caught herself up short. *"Follow my lead."* Wasn't that what she'd said? The man was only doing what she'd told him to do. But he was enjoying himself entirely too much.

Casey chuckled. "I'd be careful if I was you, boy."

"That's all right, Gramps. Mitch is . . ." For some reason, the word seemed to stick in her throat. She coughed it up. "Right."

"He is?"

"I am?"

Laughing, Logan ran up the hill ahead of the men. "See you two at breakfast. I need some calamine for these bites."

Mitch hung back, letting Casey set the pace as they climbed the steep slope from lakefront to lodge. The old man broke the silence between them as Logan disappeared through the front door.

" 'Skeeter bites, eh? Huh! Not like our Lily to be forgettin' the repellent."

Our Lily. Mitch couldn't deny he liked the sound of that. But

Casey was obviously fishing and he had no intention of taking the bait. "She's been away a lot of years. I'd say it's understandable."

"Ya would, would ya, boy?" Casey stopped in the middle of the path and turned to face him. "So . . . did ya kiss her?"

For the second time in less than ten minutes, Mitch felt his jaw drop. But before he could stammer a reply, the old man had lifted his cane and delivered a sharp jab to his solar plexus. "Oof! Hey! What'd you do that for?"

Casey grinned. "Just checkin', is all."

"Checkin' what?"

"Well, boy, I figured if yer intentions weren't on the up and up, you'd have been expectin' that."

Intentions? Mitch uttered a groan of defeat. "Old man, *you're* the one who said we should get to know each other better."

Chuckling, Casey turned back to the path and resumed his slow progress up the hill. "Said it and meant it, my boy. So . . . did ya kiss her?"

"She was telling me about Ryan, our summer help."

"She was, was she? And . . . ?"

Mitch tugged at the suddenly too-tight collar of his T-shirt. The old man was fishing all right; he could practically feel the hook in his mouth! One way or another, Logan was going to pay for leaving him alone to face the inquisition. "And . . . she said he's a bit of a smart aleck."

"Most are at that age. Don't mean he's not a good kid, though. Then what?"

Don't answer. Right. The conversation with Logan was private—nobody's business but their own. He had every right to turn his back and walk away. But he didn't—couldn't.

Instead, Mitch watched as his old friend struggled to climb the three steps to the dining room door. He knew better than to offer assistance. Casey would do it by himself, as usual, relying on his cane and the strength that came from seventy years of hard work. The old guy was still as stubborn as ever. Full of love for his family, too. *And hasn't he always made you feel like one of the family?*

Mitch shoved both hands into his pockets and bowed his head. Turning his back on Casey O'Malley would be like turning his back on his own father . . . assuming he had a father, that is.

He drew a deep breath for courage. "And then . . ." *Just say it!* "Then I told her about Alison. And I told her she'd better be really sure of what she wants before . . . well, you know."

Casey paused, one hand on the screen door, and looked back over his shoulder. His eyes were wide with surprise. "You said that, boy?"

Mitch nodded, grinning broadly as he reached past to shove the screen door open. Apparently Casey hadn't expected to hook the big one. Now that he had, revenge was in sight.

One way or another, Logan was going to pay for leaving him alone to face the inquisition.

What better way than to leave her grandfather with a little ammunition for his favorite pastime—teasing Lily.

"And that, old man, is when I kissed her."

Chapter Thirteen

"*N*_{o! Oh! Yieeeee—!"}

Logan's shriek was cut short, first by the shock of cold water, then by the natural instinct to shut her mouth before she swallowed half of Thembi.

She opened her eyes to a watery world, an icy, crystal blue, asparkle with reflected sunlight. Despite a full week of sunny days, the lake was still cold enough to raise instant gooseflesh on her body. Logan felt her Jays cap float away as her long hair fanned out around her shoulders and drifted, like auburn strands of seaweed, in front of her eyes.

Laced into a pair of heavy work boots, her feet sank like a couple of rocks, tipping her upright almost immediately. Seconds later she surfaced, neck deep in frigid water, sputtering, coughing, and grabbing for her cap. Looking up, she found Mitch grinning at her from the end of the dock. True to his word, the man had managed to collect on their berry-picking bet when she'd least expected it.

She crooked a finger at him, already shivering so hard her teeth rattled. "C-come on in. Water's f-fine."

Mitch's grin spread ear-to-ear. "Sure looks fine on you, lady. But I think I'll pass this time."

"*Ch-chicken?*"

"That's right. I'm a nice, *warm*, sun-baked chicken. And your debt is paid in full."

137

Warm and sunbaked? We'll see about that. "Looks to me as if the chicken needs basting!"

She sent a hatful of water flying in his direction, but quickly thought better of waiting to see if she'd hit her mark, wading ashore as fast as her water-numbed legs would carry her. She broke into a run when she reached the shallows, galloping up the hill and into the lodge, dribbling water across the polished pine floor of the dining room and leaving puddles on the thread-bare carpet of the staircase. Nudging the bathroom door shut behind her, she kicked off her boots, peeled clammy shirt and shorts away from equally clammy skin, and dove into the shower. Ten minutes under the hot water should do the trick. Meanwhile, Mitch could cool his heels with no one to blame but himself for delaying their day trip to town.

She let her eyes fall shut as the hot water worked its magic, easing tense muscles and freeing her mind to wander. Seven days of hard work in the fresh air and sunshine had taken their toll, left her too weary to do more than dream about her blossoming feelings for Mitch, although Gramps had taken great joy in teasing her about what he *thought* was going on between them. And the more she'd denied it, the more gleeful the old man's teasing had become. Where on earth could he have gotten the idea she'd been kissing Mitch? Not that she'd object to giving it a try! But, so far, "almost" was as close as they'd come . . . unless you counted that morning in the rowboat when he'd kissed her fingertips. . . .

Unconsciously, Logan lifted her hand, brushed those kissed fingers across her lips, and smiled. No, she wouldn't object one bit to giving it a try. But, in truth, the few precious moments she and Mitch had spent together since their morning on the lake had been decidedly *un*romantic.

Each night, once the dinner dishes were done, the two of them had met across the kitchen table to drink a second, and some-times third, cup of coffee, hash out the week's priorities, and share news of the day's accomplishments—partners in business, but *not* in romance. Ruby and Casey had joined them once or twice, but it seemed the two old friends had made a habit of playing gin rummy in the evenings so, most nights, they'd disappear into Ruby's sitting room, leaving the kitchen to "the youngsters."

Although she was scarcely aware it had happened, Logan's few lingering doubts about Mitch and his intentions had long since been banished to the farthest corners of her mind, all but forgotten as their busy days raced by.

She opened her eyes, studied her fingertips, and picked at a stubborn fleck of royal blue paint still clinging to her thumbnail. Mitch wasn't likely to want to kiss her hands again any time soon, stained and work-roughened as they were. But he'd seemed pretty pleased to see twelve of Casey's Muskoka chairs sporting fresh coats of paint—six red and six blue. And painting wasn't the only chore Logan had tackled. She'd taken over Gramps's guide duty for last weekend's fishing guests, too, earning kudos when all four men netted their limit of trophy-sized lake trout. As Gramps always said, "Happy guests are worth a whole lot more'n fancy advertisin'."

With Logan to take care of their guests, Casey had found time to finish the plumbing and electrical work at the new cabin, and Mitch had done a spectacular job with the dock, finishing just this morning. Perhaps if she hadn't been so busy oohing and ahhing over it, she might have avoided the dunking. But when Mitch gallantly invited her to be the first to stroll its length, she'd accepted the honor with pleasure, never suspecting the devious ulterior motive lurking behind his charming smile.

She gave the tap a twist and reached for her towel, chuckling to herself as she rubbed the last of the chills away. Just as well Mitch had collected his due before Ryan arrived from Toronto. The kid probably would've leaped to her rescue and, somehow, she couldn't imagine trying to explain how a basket of raspberries had earned his sane and sensible teacher a swim in the cold lake.

Snuggling the bath towel around her, Logan tossed her sodden clothes over the shower bar and made a dash for her room, suddenly in a hurry to get their trip under way. It had taken half a dozen radio-to-phone relays via Bales's Marine, but the details for Ryan's employment had at last been finalized and their eager summer helper was due to arrive in Red Lake on the late afternoon bus. She and Mitch planned to meet him there after a day of running errands in Indigo Bay. Thanks to Casey and Ruby, their to-do list was almost as long as the new dock.

"First on the list, pick up my summer clothes," she said aloud, pulling on a clean pair of jeans and grimacing as she shrugged into a rainbow tie-dyed T-shirt—a relic from the summer she turned fifteen. As promised, Mitch had brought back two of the crates they'd had to leave in storage at Bales's Marine. But with the Beaver filled to capacity with guests and luggage on one trip, and loaded to the struts with bulky, black plastic floats for the new dock on the next, he'd been forced to leave one of her boxes behind. Didn't it just figure it was the one with all her summer things inside? She was getting a bit tired of wearing bright pink and purple, and having a *really* hard time believing she'd ever actually *liked* the stuff—no wonder Auntie Pearl had insisted on outfitting her "properly" the minute they'd arrived in the city.

"Well, at least it still fits. Sort of." She tugged on the hem of the shirt and grimaced again, into the mirror this time, then made a halfhearted job of brushing her hair, finally twisting it into a knot at the nape of her neck. Leaving her Blue Jays cap on the bedpost to dry, she shoved her bare feet into a comfortable pair of navy deck shoes and went looking for Mitch. She'd kept him waiting long enough.

*   *   *

Too bad she wasn't in the market for a little revenge. Standing only inches from the edge of the dock, Mitch seemed thoroughly preoccupied with his preflight check and hadn't yet noticed her approach.

"Just about ready?"

He straightened abruptly at the sound of her voice, reaching for a handhold as he spun to face her. "Uh, yeah. Almost."

Logan grinned as he latched onto the wing strut. Maybe she wasn't the only one who'd had thoughts of a watery revenge. She raised her hands in a gesture of surrender. "Don't worry, I'm declaring a truce. Have you pumped out the floats yet?"

"Nope." Mitch climbed up onto the plane's nose to check the oil levels. "That's next up and then we're outta here."

Without a second thought, Logan picked the hand pump out of Mitch's tool kit and went to work, quickly clearing the back float chamber of water. It never occurred to her, until she glanced up from her work and discovered him watching, that perhaps she should have asked him if he *wanted* help. The man looked more than a little astonished.

"You don't mind, I hope?"

Mitch shook his head. "You're just full of surprises, aren't you, Lily?"

Lily. It wasn't the first time he'd used Gramps's term of endearment. At first it had seemed strange, but now . . . now she had to admit she was starting to like the way it sounded. "Surprises keep life interesting. And there's still a lot you don't know about me, Mitchell Walker."

"Is that so?"

"Mmm-hmm. I've been around floatplanes all my life, you know." Shifting to the next section of float, Logan resumed her pumping. "Even flown a few times. Not solo, but Walt said I was close to ready. Maybe we could pick up where he left off. What do you think?"

The words had barely left her mouth before Logan regretted

them. It was too soon. Things between them had relaxed, sure, but asking the man to trust her with his airplane, his Old Beauty . . . It was too much, too fast.

Apparently Mitch thought so, too. He was strangely quiet for a moment, then jumped down from his perch on the plane's nose and began stowing his equipment. "Good old Walt. Still can't believe he packed it all in for a condo in Florida. Casey's still shaking his head over that one."

Logan shot a sideways glance in his direction. "Pretty neat change of subject, Walker."

"What do you mean?"

"I don't *really* expect you to let me fly your airplane, if that's what you're worried about." Logan pumped a little harder. Mitch stayed silent. Apparently she'd guessed exactly right. She imagined him mentally scrambling for ways to protect his precious floatplane from the city girl.

"Logan?" His hand closed around hers as he leaned close. "You're pumping air."

Wonderful. Of all times to let her mind wander. She should've been paying attention.

Mitch took the pump from her hand, dropping it onto the dock as he pulled her to her feet. "Help me turn her around, then climb aboard, okay? I'll pump out the other float."

He stopped her before she could reach for the tether line, tightening his grip on her hand. "Y'know, this Old Beauty's been mine for nearly seven years, and in all that time, *nobody's* flown her but me."

"Yeah. I kind of figured that." She stifled a sigh. She'd known all along how protective he was of the floatplane. His reaction was exactly what she'd expected. What she *hadn't* counted on was feeling so disappointed. No need to let it show, though. "I do understand, really. I never should have suggested—"

He laughed—a warm, gentle sort of laugh that soothed her

wounded pride as surely as a touch. When he tenderly cupped
her chin in his hand and tipped her face upward, she found that
same warmth and gentleness shining deep within his blue eyes.

"Thing is," he continued, "I never had a partner before who
wanted to give it a try."

"You . . . I . . . b-but . . ." Logan stammered and stopped,
suddenly finding it difficult to breathe, let alone speak. She
thought she'd asked the impossible. Was he really and truly
considering it? His amused expression said yes. More important,
his slow, thoughtful nod said "I trust you."

"Really?"

"Don't rush me, now." Mitch narrowed his eyes, tightened
his lips in a mock frown. "But, yeah . . . if you check out, I
don't see why not."

After a long moment of breathless amazement, Logan raised
her left hand, solemnly placing her right palm over her heart.
"I won't rush you. I promise." Grinning, she added, "But I
will check out!"

Indigo Bay didn't look much different at high noon than it had
at the crack of dawn the day she'd arrived from Toronto—a
quiet, sleepy, dusty little frontier town. Shoving her hands into
the pockets of her jeans, Logan strolled up Main Street, moving
at a leisurely pace, enjoying the warmth of the sun on her head
and reveling in the comfortable sense of homecoming. Things
had changed so little in the ten years she'd been gone, it felt as
if she'd stepped back in time. She glanced down at her shirt and
gave a barely audible groan. Even her clothes were the same.

The Aurora's blue neon sign flickered lazily in the window
as she passed, still missing its "B." A couple of scrawny-
looking dogs played tag in the street while an old man napped
on the bench in front of the general store.

A short while ago, Mitch and Logan had been the store's only
customers. The two of them had parted ways once Ruby's list

of supplies had been purchased and stowed aboard the plane. Mitch had some *AirWalker* business to take care of, including the rescue of her summer crate from Bales' storeroom, so Logan had decided to take a walk through town and do a little reminiscing.

Ten years gone, and nothing had changed. But only ten days home and her world was a much different place. She'd never felt happier or more content. Coming back to the north, to Casey Lodge, Gramps, Ruby . . . *and Mitch* . . . was the best decision she'd made in a very long time.

Soon Ryan would be a part of their lodge family, too, working and playing the way she had as a teenager, learning about the possibilities of life beyond the city. When he returned to school in September, he'd take memories to last a lifetime, horizons broad enough to hold a dream, and the confidence to make his dream come true. She thought about how much her young student had in common with Mitch and let herself smile. She couldn't have asked for a better role model for the boy.

If things worked out, they'd bring two or three kids up next summer, maybe more the year after. And that's when her own dreams would start coming true, because she'd know she was making a difference in their young lives.

She stopped in front of the post office, and smiled and nodded at the leather-faced old man who'd just pushed through the door clutching a handful of mail.

" 'Mornin'," he said, shuffling past. "Or is it afternoon? Beautiful day, eh?"

"Sure is."

"Darn shame about the fires."

"Fires? What . . . ?" Logan felt suddenly cold, as if Thembi's frigid waters had claimed her once again and were pulling her down.

"West," said the old man, pointing a gnarled finger in that direction. "Lookin' like another bad 'un. Jacob's got it on the radio inside.'' He shook his head sadly. ''Couple more south of us, too. They're like to do some real damage this time. Darn shame.''

Logan watched the old man shuffle across the street and disappear into the cool, dark interior of the general store. Wrapping her arms tightly around her waist, she scanned the sky. No trace of smoke, just an endless expanse of blue. Not surprising. The day was so calm, Mitch had been worried about losing too much lift when they landed the float.

Mitch. Did he know about the fires? He must. He'd had the headset on all the way down from Casey Lodge. She remembered thinking he looked worried a couple of times, but when she'd caught his eye, he'd smiled so cheerfully, she'd put it down to her imagination. Why hadn't he told her? Did he think he was protecting her by keeping quiet?

Turning, she pulled open the post office door and hurried inside. Gramps would never forgive her if she came home without his mail, and maybe this ''Jacob'' the old man had mentioned would tell her a bit more about the fires.

It was cool in the vestibule, a pleasant contrast to the warmth of the noonday sun. Dust motes hung in the still air and the place smelled faintly musty, reminding her of the third-floor storeroom at the school, back in Toronto. She smiled. Even the smells hadn't changed in Indigo Bay. No wonder that particular room at school had always felt so eerily familiar.

Logan's smile became a frown when she saw the sign on the inner door. OUT TO LUNCH. ''Well, darn.''

Crossing her arms over her chest, she turned to lean heavily against the wall. Gramps would have to do without his mail after all, she thought, scuffing at the graying tile floor with the toe of her shoe. And she'd have to do without more details on the fire because, unless Jacob took really short lunch hours, she and Mitch would be long gone before he got back. ''Darn.''

She'd pushed away from the wall and taken a couple of steps

toward the exit before she saw it—an expensive-looking brass plaque, polished until it gleamed, looking strangely out of place on a time-worn door painted the same institutional green as the rest of the old building's interior. D'OR-ON EXPLORATIONS, it said, in flowing cursive script. ONTARIO-NORTHLAND DIVISION. She frowned thoughtfully. Apparently not everything in Indigo Bay had stayed the same.

With no idea of what she'd do once inside, Logan crossed the vestibule, twisted the knob, and pushed the door open, just wide enough to slip through. The tiny office appeared deserted. To her left, under the window, sat three folding chairs. Two of them were empty. The third held a stack of dog-eared magazines and a half-empty Styrofoam coffee cup. The room smelled faintly of new carpet, but that minor amenity, a nondescript, industrial beige twist, was obviously the extent of the management's attempt at redecorating.

Opposite the door, a wooden counter spanned the width of the room, its surface hidden beneath an assortment of laminated topographic maps. In a brief flash of déjà vu, Logan remembered standing at the counter as a child, barely able to see over the top. She was holding Gramps's hand, hopping from one foot to the other, impatient to be on their way, eager to go home and help him open all the packages . . .

Of course. Now she remembered. D'Or-On had taken over the old Catalogue Shopping Depot. She moved slowly across the room, stopping to run her hand along the curved edge of the counter, worn smooth from the touch of many hands before hers.

A large map, mounted on the wall at the end of the counter and sprouting a multicolored assortment of plastic pushpins, drew Logan's attention back to the present. The territory was familiar and almost immediately she picked out the crooked finger outline of Thembi. A field of red pins bristled around Casey Lodge property. She moved closer, uncomfortably aware of her suddenly dry mouth and knotted stomach. Those flags weren't *around* lodge property, at all. They were *on* it.

"Can I help you?"

Slowly, Logan turned to face the speaker, a slender young man with faded brown hair and faded brown eyes to match. He watched her curiously, peering out at her through equally faded tortoiseshell glasses.

"Kip Douglas," he said, smiling as he rested his elbows on the counter. "Chief geologist. Anything I can help you with?"

Logan realized she'd been staring at him and smiled sweetly. "Logan Paris. Not really. I've been away for a while, and . . . I'm just curious about all this." She made a sweeping gesture toward the map, then homed in on Indigo Bay with one finger. "We're here, right?"

"That's right. And all the flags are registered claims."

"Wow!" She flashed him an admiring smile. "Your company sure has a lot of land staked out. Hmm, isn't this Casey Lodge?" Standing on tiptoes, Logan tapped the surface of the map, just below the cluster of red pins.

"Casey Lodge?" Kip squinted and frowned. "Never heard of— Oh, you mean the Walker Place."

Logan's breath caught in her throat. "The *Walker* place?"

"Yeah, Mitch Walker. A real go-getter. Got himself a sweet deal goin' up there, for sure."

"If somebody wanted to, it'd be pretty easy to take advantage of Casey." The room seemed to swim around her as every doubt, every question she'd ever had about Mitch filled her mind in a dizzying rush.

She steadied herself, gripping the edge of the counter with both hands and pasting on a smile she hoped would fool Kip, who was now studying her with unabashed interest.

"I used to spend summers up there with my grandfather. Any idea what Mr. Walker's planning to do with the old place?"

Kip shrugged. "Dunno. But if there's gold in them thar hills, he's gonna be one rich hombre.'' He smiled at his own joke and pushed away from the counter. ''Would you like to see the claim records?''

''You have copies?''

''Well, sure. It's all public record.''

''Might be interesting, Kip. I've never seen claim records before.''

As Kip turned and pulled open a file drawer, Logan felt her smile begin to wobble and her confidence with it. Hadn't Mitch told her he was staking the land in Gramps's name, for him . . . for her? Maybe Kip was mistaken. Maybe he knew Mitch had done the paperwork and just assumed . . .

''Miss? Are you all right?''

Passing her hand across her eyes, Logan struggled to regain her composure. Numbly, she stared down at the papers Kip had fanned across the counter between them. The O'Malley name was conspicuously absent, while Mitchell Walker's seemed to leap off the pages, mocking her.

Her mind reeled with thoughts of the time she and Mitch had spent together, all the plans they'd made, his smile, the touch of his lips on her fingertips. Why would he lie? Unless . . .

Was all the warmth and tenderness just a sham? Were the gentle smiles and playful teasing just a ploy to win her trust, to capture her love . . . to keep her from discovering the truth?

Her stomach lurched. Tears burned behind her eyes and she longed to give in, let them flow, run away from this place and find Mitch, confront him, demand an explanation . . . beg him to convince her she was wrong.

But Mitch had already proven his skill at convincing her. No, this time she'd take her proof to Gramps. The old man might be getting on in years, but he was no fool. He'd know what to do about the claim on their land and the man who'd betrayed their trust. But would he know how to mend his granddaughter's broken heart?

"Miss?"

"Kip, I—I'm sorry. Must've been out in the sun too long. Could I trouble you for a glass of water?"

"Oh, sure, sure." He patted her hand, looking genuinely concerned. "You just wait right here."

Beyond the counter, a doorway opened onto the rest of the D'Or-On operation and Kip hurried through, giving her one last worried glance, as if he thought she might fall over.

She worked up a reassuring smile. "I'll be fine, really."

As he disappeared around the corner, Logan slipped a single claim form out of the sheaf of documents he'd presented, crumpling it into a ball as she shoved it into the pocket of her jeans. She barely had time to fold her hands on the counter again before Kip returned, carrying her glass of water.

"Here you go . . . Logan, is it?"

She nodded weakly, then gasped as he pressed the glass into her hand, splashing water onto the counter top *and* the remaining claim forms.

"Aw, don't worry about that," said Kip, sweeping it away with the side of his hand. "They're only copies."

Logan breathed a guilty sigh as she sipped the water. Once this whole mess was over and done with, she'd make sure Kip got copies of the *real* claim forms, the ones with O'Malley on the dotted line.

"Feeling better?" Kip leaned close, resting his hand on hers. "Would you like to come in the back and sit down?"

Logan straightened, extricating her hand to smooth her shirt and tuck a stray wisp of hair behind her ear. "No, I should be going. But thanks . . . for everything."

"Don't run off. I was thinking . . . that is . . . well, I'm new in town, don't know too many people yet and . . . would you like to get together, y'know, for dinner or something? I hear the Aurora makes a great prime rib."

Logan's already queasy stomach lurched at the thought. "Sorry, Kip, I can't."

He looked genuinely disappointed. Nudging the faded tortoiseshell glasses into place with one finger, he gave her a melancholy smile. "Don't date geologists, eh?"

"No, it's not that. I'm sure dinner would be lovely. But, you see, I'm already . . ." She stumbled over the word, stung by the realization of how dramatically—how *painfully*—its meaning had changed in only ten minutes. "I'm already involved."

Chapter Fourteen

"That you, Logan?"

She glared at his back, balled her hands into tight, angry fists, and willed a note of normalcy into her voice. This wasn't the time or place to confront him with what she knew.

"Yeah, it's me."

"Glad you're back. Hand me those bungee cords, will you?"

Logan climbed through the open cargo door, bracing herself against one of the passenger seats as the floatplane bobbed, then settled again on the water. She scanned the floor, quickly locating the elastic cords Mitch had asked for, scooping them up and dropping them into his outstretched hand. Thank goodness he hadn't bothered to turn around. She'd never been any good at hiding her emotions and it seemed her body wasn't about to start cooperating now. Heart pounding, teeth clenched, mouth as dry as the dust on Main Street, she pictured herself pinch-cheeked and ghostly pale. One glance in her direction and the man would *know* something was wrong.

She squared her shoulders, tried to force herself to relax, but as she watched him secure the last of their cargo, carefully checking and rechecking each span of rope and elastic, she felt the already-painful knot in her stomach begin to tighten.

"Gotta love this Old Beauty," he said, giving one last tug on the corner of her summer crate. "Even with the seats in, she packs one heck of a payload."

Mitch's satisfied smile faded the instant he turned around. "Logan? What's wrong?"

His hand settled over hers before she could think to pull away. Unconsciously, she'd been gripping the seatback, holding fast to that little piece of familiar reality, an anchor in her storm of emotions. Now, as he stroked her fingers, Logan felt her precarious hold on rational behavior beginning to slip. Anger warred with pain and, burning bright in the middle of it all, a tiny glimmer of hope that maybe, just maybe, she was wrong.

Despite the balled-up wad of paper in her pocket—her absolute, black-and-white proof of Mitch Walker's sins—part of her still wanted to believe in him. Part of her still could not conceive of how this gentle, thoughtful man had earned her trust, won her love so quickly and so completely, only to betray her and everything he claimed to believe in.

She turned away, reclaiming her hand, wrapping her arms tightly around her waist. Beyond the door was a world of blue skies and sunshine, singing birds and leaping fish. Home. For the first time in ten days, Logan felt out of place and ill at ease.

"Logan . . . ?"

"What's wrong?" He was still expecting an answer. Well, *everything* just about covered it. "Nothing. I'm fine. Just a bit of a headache, that's all."

"You know, don't you?"

She stiffened. How could he possibly have guessed?

"I was going to tell you myself, but . . ."

Logan knew he was shrugging, even without turning to look at him. She could picture the slow roll of his shoulders, the palms-up gesture he made with his hands, the wide-eyed, innocent expression. She'd come to know him so well in ten days. So well, and yet not at all.

". . . it seemed kind of pointless, y'know? I mean, I knew you'd just worry."

His voice sounded hollow, empty except for a touch of . . . Of what? Regret? Of course. He regretted getting caught.

"Worry?" At last she turned to face him, letting disbelief color her voice. "You knew I'd *worry?*"

"Okay, okay, settle down." He made a calming gesture with his hands as he moved toward her. Too close for comfort, but Logan had nowhere else to go. Behind her, the open doorway yawned on a five foot drop to the dock.

Mitch's hands settled lightly on her shoulders. "Why don't you tell me what you already know?"

She felt suddenly cold, as if Thembi's frigid water were running in her veins. Mitch responded to her involuntary shiver by pulling her close, folding his arms around her, resting his chin on the top of her head. Last night she'd dreamed of his embrace, but now . . .

Her stomach lurched in protest.

"I'm sorry." He held her even closer, stroking her hair with his hand. "That was a dumb question. You heard talk about how bad the fires are this time, right?"

The fires. Breath caught in her throat. They'd been talking about two different things. She nodded mutely, let her head rest briefly on Mitch's chest as anger gave way to an odd combination of relief and dread. He had no idea what she'd discovered. But the fires . . . She'd actually let herself forget about the fires.

She pulled away, sank onto one of the passenger seats, drew her knees up in front of her like a shield. "How bad?"

"Flare-ups where Andy thought they had everything under control, and two new ones—*big* ones, farther south."

"You spoke to Andy?"

"No, I talked to the Fire Boss. Andy's kinda busy right now. They moved his crew to Camp Seven, a ridge to the east of where we saw him last week. They're cutting a fire break, trying to protect the First Nations settlement at Bear River. If things go according to plan, though, the fire won't get that far.''

''Water bombers?''

Mitch nodded, slouching onto the seat opposite hers. ''Yeah, the bombers made a couple of runs but they're needed down south. Too bad they couldn't stick around and finish the job. Should help, though, damp things off a bit, maybe slow it down. They're doing some pretty aggressive clearing, too.''

He frowned, spiking his fingers through his hair before meeting her gaze again. ''Fire Boss put us on notice, Logan. Me an' the Old Beauty. But he says they're in pretty good shape supply-wise this time, so unless something goes wrong, we'll have plenty of time to get Ryan and make the trip back to Thembi.''

Logan wrapped her arms around her knees and held tight. *''Unless something goes wrong ...''* She knew he was only trying to be helpful, but his words filled her with a sense of doom. Predicting forest fire behavior was guesswork at best, or so it had always seemed to her. She squeezed her eyes shut, battling tears and a new flood of emotions that threatened to overwhelm her. Just moments ago, she'd been so full of anger, eager to banish Mitch from her life forever. So why did the thought of sending him back into the fire zone fill her with such terror?

''I wonder ... does Ruby know? She'll be worried about Andy.''

''I talked to your Gramps on the CB a while ago. Figured I oughta fill them in before they started seeing the smoke.''

Logan looked over her shoulder at the patch of blue sky framed by the open cargo door. A gray smudge hung low on the western horizon, still faint enough that she might have missed it if she hadn't known what to look for. Turning back, she forced her chin high and met Mitch's gaze. ''And when did you plan on telling me?''

''Not until I had to.'' Mitch reached across the narrow aisle to caress her cheek with one finger, then let his hand settle gently over hers. "We should get going." He gave a reassuring squeeze. "It'll be okay. There's no threat to the lodge—not yet, anyway. And don't forget, we had rain a couple of nights. The forest isn't as dry around Thembi as it is a little farther south."

She nodded, unable to look away. He was studying her intently, eyes full of compassion, a gentle, loving warmth that left her aching to feel his arms around her again. Straightening her legs, she pushed stiffly to her feet, slipping her hand into the pocket of her jeans to touch the crumpled sheet of paper. Her proof. A bitter reminder of misplaced trust and shattered dreams.

Drawing a deep breath, Logan mustered what she hoped was a brave smile. "Don't look so worried. Wasn't it you who said fires are a part of life up here?"

He nodded. "Yes, but—"

"No. No buts. Let's just go, okay? I'll cope. I'll be fine."

Mitch studied the floor for a moment, then met her gaze again. "I know you will."

His confident smile was almost enough to make her believe she could really do it. Much more of this, and she'd be falling into his arms again without any effort at all on his part. She pushed past him, sinking into her seat in the cockpit and pulling the shoulder harness into place.

"Not so fast," said Mitch, dropping an orange Bales' Marine bag into her lap. "Thought you might need this."

Logan poked gingerly at the bag. "Not more wet towels, I hope."

"No, not more wet towels." Mitch folded himself into the pilot's seat, winking as he added, "I did stow some under your seat, though, just in case."

Groaning at the prospect of another smoky flight, Logan opened the bag and peered inside. "What . . . ? I don't understand."

''Your own headset. I figured you'd need it if you're serious about flying the Old Beauty some day.''

Serious? A few hours ago, his willingness to let her try had meant the world to her. But now . . .

Logan shifted uneasily, aware of the balled-up claim form pressing like a thorn against her hip. She slipped two fingers into her pocket and pulled the paper free, hiding it in her tightly clenched fist. With the other hand, she lifted the sleek headset out of the bag and held it up.

''I . . . I don't know what to say.''

''Say thank you and plug yourself in.'' Mitch finished his preflight check by flashing a smile in her direction. ''We're outta here, partner!''

''That's Camp Seven, where Andy is, right?'' Logan jabbed at the chart with her finger, locating a tiny lake, sheltered on its west by a long, narrow ridge. ''About five minutes away?''

Mitch nodded, his forehead creased with worry, as if he knew exactly what she was about to suggest and didn't like it one bit. Well, she wasn't too crazy about the idea herself, but what choice did they have?

''We're the closest available plane, Mitch. Even factoring in a stop to unload all this stuff at Camp Seven, you can get to those men twenty minutes sooner than anyone else.''

''And what about you? There are six of them, Logan—a full house.''

''I'll stay with Andy. It'll be okay. Mitch, we *don't* have a choice!''

His stricken expression tugged mightily at her conscience. Clearly the man knew what had to be done, and she knew him well enough to be certain the rescue would already be under way, if not for her.

If not for her. How could she possibly doubt his feelings?

Wrong. She glanced down at her hand, at five fingers still curled around a crumpled sheet of paper. *The Walker Place.* It wasn't his feelings she needed to question, but the motives behind them. Not now, though. Right now, what they needed was action.

"Just do it, Mitch!"

His resigned sigh seemed to hang in the air between them. Despite the drone of the Beaver's engine, she could have have sworn she'd actually heard it twice—once through the headset and once from across the aisle. Mitch brushed the backs of his fingers down her cheek before he finally nodded agreement. "I'll make the call."

"And Ryan . . . what about Ryan?"

"Bales has a sister in Red Lake. I'll give him a call, too, ask him to have her meet the boy at the bus. He'll be fine, Logan. Don't worry."

Don't worry. Logan dragged the headset off her ears and let it drop into her lap, unwilling to endure yet another report on the harsh realities of the fire. She'd heard enough already to rouse the old memories and send her thoughts spinning earthward.

After an unusually dry spring and several weeks of warm weather, the forests across most of northwestern Ontario were tinderbox dry. Not long ago—it must've been just about the time Kip Douglas and his claim records had turned her own world upside down—things had gone dangerously wrong out on the fire lines. At last count, there'd been three more flare-ups in the area around Lake Opakopa, and a sudden, gusty wind out of the west had left one crew stranded in the path of a raging wildfire.

Only half an hour into their flight to Red Lake, they'd heard the plea for help from the area Fire Boss. Several other small planes had responded, but all were at least an hour away from the trapped crew. Mitch was their best, possibly their *only,* hope.

Logan edged forward in her seat, focusing on the horizon and three billowing columns of smoke. As she watched, the three gradually became one, a great, black, sun-swallowing cloud. Squeezing her eyes shut, she tried to banish the haunting memory of flames and fear . . . the same fear those trapped fire fighters had to be feeling.

"Mitch?" She grabbed the headset, jamming it carelessly onto her head once again, feeling breathless and edgy as she spoke his name into the mouthpiece. "Mitch? How much longer?"

With a wordless gesture below, he began their descent toward Camp Seven—a lake so tiny she wondered how they'd ever manage to land on its blue-green surface. Drifting smoke swirled around the plane as they sank lower, not dense and blinding like last time, but enough to fill the cockpit with an eye-smarting haze.

"You okay?" Mitch touched her arm as he spoke, gentle as always.

"Fine." *What a lie!* Their swift downward spiral seemed the perfect mirror for the dizzying rush of emotion she struggled to contain. She'd begun to realize the fear she was feeling was as much for Mitch as for herself. She told herself he was a good, experienced pilot. He'd flown around, over, even through fires before, and this time was no different. He'd rescue the trapped men and fly them to safety. He'd be okay. He'd . . .

What if he doesn't come back? Her fist tightened around the hopelessly crumpled claim form, still hidden in her hand. Should she ask him about it now, get things out in the open between them while she still had the chance?

"Kilo-Mike-X-ray to Camp Seven." His voice droned in her ear, a strangely intimate sensation, as if he was there with her, inside her head. She remembered the first day they met, marveling at how he always seemed to know what she was thinking, wondering if the man could read her mind.

"Come in, Camp Seven. Kilo-Mike-X-ray, just off the water. We're gonna need some help unloading."

But Mitch Walker was no mind reader. He was only a man. A man she'd felt certain cared as much for her as she did for him.

As the Beaver settled lightly onto the water, another familiar voice echoed in her ear. "Seven to Kilo-Mike. Hey, Mitch, let's get this show on the road, man."

Despite his easy manner, Logan could hear the tension in Andy Twelvetrees's voice. Like her, he had to be imagining what those six stranded men were going through.

"We're on the water," answered Mitch. "Can you spare a couple of men to give me a hand?"

" 'Fraid not. You'll hafta make do with me."

"Make do?"

"Shortstuff? That you?"

"Sure is. But the Andy I remember used to say he was worth at least two *ordinary* men."

Logan felt her own tension ease a little when Andy laughed.

"Yeah, well, not anymore. I'm up to three now. Four on a good day. I hear you're gonna keep me company for a while."

"Yeah. Thought you might need some help."

"You did, eh? Well—"

"Let's just get the Old Beauty unloaded, okay? You two can visit later."

"Yes, *sir*. On the job, *sir*." Andy's crisp delivery made it easy to imagine him saluting as he spoke the words, but Mitch's only response was a scowl. Surely he wasn't jealous of her easygoing relationship with Ruby's son?

Andy emerged from the forest to sprint across the narrow beach, a flash of brilliant yellow in his Fire Service coveralls. He stopped at the water's edge and waved, then raised his handset and spoke to them once more. "Go ahead and beach her, man. There's nothin' here but weeds and sand."

"Roger," said Mitch, cutting the engine, letting the plane glide swift and silent toward the beach . . . and Andy. The big man jumped and hustled out of their way as sand and water whooshed against the metal floats. Mitch was out the door almost before they'd stopped, walking along the float to open the cargo door, admitting a smoke-heavy breeze that tangled Logan's hair as she pulled the headset off and stowed it under her seat.

"Yo, Shortstuff! Whatcha sittin' around for?" Andy poked his head through the door and grinned. "You okay?"

"I'm fine. And I'm *not* 'sittin' around'!"

She pushed to her feet just as Mitch climbed through the cargo door. He paused to give her a dubious frown that she quickly discovered was a pretty close match for the one Andy was wearing.

"All right, you guys, cut it out. I said I'm fine and I meant it. Stop worrying about me, okay? Let's just get this done."

Ignoring the woebegone glances the two men exchanged, Logan moved quickly into the back of the plane and began releasing the ropes and bungee cords that held their cargo in place. Unloading would be much quicker and easier here than it had been at Opakopa with its steep, rocky shoreline and jagged, pontoon-bending boulders. And if they were lucky, the little plane would float itself free once the weight of the cargo had been removed.

The three of them worked quickly, clearing the plane of several boxes of groceries and household supplies, half a dozen bundles of shingles for Casey's new cabin, and Logan's ill-fated summer crate. As she'd hoped, the much-lightened Beaver was floating in several inches of water once they'd finished.

She and Mitch closed the cargo door and turned the plane around for takeoff while Andy checked in with the Fire Boss. His expression was grim as he signed off. "You'd better move, man. Boss says things are lookin' bad."

Ankle deep in cold water, Logan felt an unexpected rush of heat as Mitch caught her hand and pulled her close. His arms slid around her, warm and strong, as he bent to brush her lips with his. Then, suddenly, he was gone, striding away from her, climbing aboard the plane. She finally found her voice when he paused in the doorway to look back at her.

"Be careful, Mitch."

"You, too. And don't worry. I'll be back before you know it." He looked past her, fixing Andy in a stern gaze. "Take care of her, Twelvetrees."

He didn't wait for an answer, turning his back on them as he settled into the pilot's seat.

"Hey!" Logan's shout stopped him with his hand on the door. "I can—"

"I know, I know . . ." Mitch sent a rueful smile her way. "You can take care of yourself."

Chapter Fifteen

"There you go, Shortstuff." Andy plunked a bright orange hardhat onto Logan's head, folded his arms across the broad expanse of his chest, and grinned approvingly. "*Now* you look like a firefighter."

She glanced down at herself and groaned. The faded yellow coveralls she'd pulled on over her jeans and T-shirt were made for someone at least twice her size. "More like a clown school reject than a f-firefighter."

Andy regarded her skeptically. "You, uh . . . you sure you're up to this?"

Logan's hands began to tremble as she tightened her belt and hitched up her sleeves. Once again, her voice and body had betrayed her. What she needed was another snappy comeback, a way to put Andy's mind at ease about this whole situation, a way to put her *own* mind at ease about what might lie ahead—for her, and for Mitch.

No. She wouldn't dwell on what *might* happen. She had a job to do in the here and now. Fresh out of snappy comebacks, Logan tipped her chin up a notch and met Andy's gaze. "I'm sure."

Hadn't her voice sounded almost steady that time, as if she believed it, as if she really was certain she could handle whatever he asked her to do? But she wasn't sure. She wasn't sure at all. "So . . . got any jobs that need doing?"

162

"About a million of 'em," said Andy, sounding utterly over-whelmed by the prospect. "But . . ."

"But what?" She did her best to work up a smile as she studied his smudged and weary face. The result was wobbly, at best.

"You're trembling."

He always was good at spotting the obvious. "Am not."

"Are too."

"Am not!" Despite her frayed nerves, it wasn't too difficult to grin back at the big bear of a man who'd fallen into their childhood banter just as easily as she.

"It's just cold feet," she said firmly, or as firmly as her still-trembly voice would allow. "And I'm not talking about me and the fire."

"Huh?"

She stomped her feet, frowning at the slightly spongy sound of her sodden deck shoes striking the hard-packed earth. "After all the sunny days we've had, I can't believe this tiny lake is still as cold as Thembi."

"Colder, I'd say."

"How's that possible?"

"Well, it's a bit like you, Shortstuff. Tiny . . . but *deep*."

His voice rumbled, dropping a tone or two on the word "deep." Logan contemplated her friend for a long moment, then made a face. "Deep?"

"Sure. You remember, don't you?"

"No, should I?"

"Mother used to tell us stories about it—Lake of Endless Water. People say there's no bottom."

"A bottomless lake? Hmm. I dunno, Andy, the bottom felt pretty solid when we were unloading those shingles a while ago."

"Oh, sure, there's a shelf near the shore. But step off—" He leaned closer, widening his eyes the way he used to when they

were kids telling scary stories. "Step off, and the earth is gone
. . . *forever.*"

"Uh-huh."

He shrugged again. "Well, *you're* the scientist. *You* explain
why it never warms up."

"Why? Well, I suppose . . . um . . . well—"

Andy's walkie-talkie buzzed and crackled, cutting short her
not-exactly-scientific reply.

"Yeah?" He bellowed the word into the mouthpiece, then
listened for a second. "Be right there—with the cavalry."

"I'm the cavalry now?"

"Closest thing we got, Shortstuff. Ready to work?"

"You bet."

Andy pointed up a steep slope. "My crew's cuttin' a firebreak
just over that ridge, and they sure could use a gofer. Y'know,
go fer this, go fer that. Mostly they'll be lookin' for gas, chainsaw oil, drinkin' water . . . Anything they need, you run back
down here and fetch it. Okay? Let's go."

Andy was off and running, sprinting halfway up the hill before she'd formed her answer. Logan shrugged. He wouldn't
have heard her, anyway. Walkie-talkie in hand, the man kept
up a steady stream of orders and encouragement for his men as
he scrambled toward the crest of the ridge.

Well, cavalry, what're you waiting for?

Grabbing a couple of canteens of fresh water and a five gallon
can of gas from the supply tent, Logan began to climb, following the same diagonal path Andy traveled, dividing her attention
between his swiftly moving back and the impossibly rough ter-
rain beneath her feet.

For such a big man, Andy Twelvetrees sure could move. The
impossibility of keeping up with him quickly became obvious,
and rather painfully so. Deck shoes were never intended for this.
Logan slipped and nearly tumbled, scraping her ankle on a rock.
The water bottles sloshed with every step, thudding against her

hips, threatening to throw her off balance again, and the gas container seemed awfully heavy, too—much heavier than it had a few moments ago. She resorted to dragging it along behind her as she traversed the slope on hands and knees.

The ridge itself was bald rock, steep and slippery. Struggling to her feet at the crest, Logan paused to catch her breath. The air was thick with smoke, alive with the buzz of chainsaws. She could see Andy's crew on the hillside below her, clearing the spindly trees that grew here and there in shallow pockets of soil, leaving logs and branches littering the clearing like a giant game of pick-up sticks. Two of the men were doing the grunt work, using pikes and chains to drag the rubble away. With luck, the strip of rock and bare earth left behind would stop the approaching fire in its tracks.

"Hey!" One of the crewmen beckoned her. "Over here. I need water!"

"Me, too!"

"Over here!"

Forget catching her breath! The supplies were instantly, and apparently endlessly, in demand. Logan ran from one worker to the next, stumbling over fallen trees and debris, until all the gas and all the water were gone.

"Be right back," she yelled, barreling up the hill and over the crest. She slid most of the way down the other side on her behind. By the third trip to the top, her body was screaming for relief. Muscles she hadn't even dreamed existed, burned with a fierce, consuming heat. Her T-shirt, drenched with sweat, clung uncomfortably to her back. She longed to stop, if only for a minute, to catch her breath, to ease the pounding of her heart. But she didn't. She wouldn't.

You can do this. Over and over, as she carried and climbed and ran, Logan repeated the words to herself. *You can do this.* If the guys on the line couldn't stop to rest, then neither could she. *Keep climbing, don't think about the fire or the danger or the pain. Don't think about Mitch. You can do this.* She was starting to believe it.

The blast of hot air struck without warning, bowling Logan off her feet, sending her scrabbling down the bald face of the rock. She dug in her heels, grabbed for the first handhold she saw, and came to a stop at Andy's feet. He had the walkie-talkie in his hand but he wasn't yelling. This time he was listening.

Logan hauled herself up off the ground. The buzz of chainsaws had stopped. Strung out along the valley floor, she saw the other five members of Andy's crew. One stood perfectly still, staring into the forest as if in a trance. The others were running.

"Move!" yelled Andy. "We got a blowup. It's coming!"

"A b-blow—?" For one blood-chilling moment, Logan stood as if frozen, staring into the distance, waiting. For what? She heard it then, a new sound, a low, mournful moan, like a far-away freight train.

"Move!"

Logan reached for the gas can.

"Leave it," ordered Andy, grabbing her shoulders to turn her toward the ridge. "Just go. Get back to the lake."

A blinding, choking haze rolled over them as he spoke, carried on a superheated wind. As if controlled by a mind of their own, her legs started to run, to climb. She could hear Andy and the crew, yelling as they scrambled up and over the ridge, but she couldn't see them. It was as if the world had vanished in a murky cloud of smoke.

She'd never felt more alone or more afraid. Would she ever see Mitch again? *I can take care of myself.* Those were the last words she'd said to him. Not "why did you do it?" Not "I love you." *I can take care of myself.* Out here, no one doubted that. Out here, she wasn't a helpless city girl, she was just one of the guys. And it was every man for himself.

As she climbed the steep hillside, the low moan in the distance became a deep, rumbling roar—and not so distant anymore. No freight train ever sounded like that. *Run faster. Keep moving. Don't stop.*

At the crest of the ridge she looked back, squinting through the smoke. In that split second a tree candled, bursting into flame from base to crown. It was no more than fifty feet beyond the firebreak. Filling her lungs with a gulp of acrid air, Logan dove for safety, rolling, sliding, out of control until she hit a tree and managed to get her feet beneath her again. She ran on, downhill now, pushing through the smoke, eyes burning, lungs on fire.

"Logan? Logan!"

Andy! She tried to shout back, tried to tell him she was all right, but found she didn't have the breath to make a sound.

"This way, Logan. Over here."

At least her feet were still working. Drawing a ragged breath, she followed the sound of his voice.

"Say again?"

The radio crackled and sputtered. Mitch was almost certain the voice was Andy's, but reception was garbled. He could only hear bits and pieces.

". . . lake . . ." said the voice. ". . . Camp Seven," and something about the fire. He heard the word "blowup," and then a frantic plea, "We need . . . bomber. Where's the water bomber?"

Mitch knew they weren't going to get their water bomber, but there was no point in telling them. Not yet, anyway.

"Twenty minutes!" he yelled. "Just hang on. I'll get you out."

No answer.

"Is Logan with you?" He held his breath, waiting. The radio crackled one last time before it died.

"No!" Mitch drove his fist into the door panel, then set about coaxing a little more speed out of the old Beaver. Pulling the stranded work crew off that lake to the north had taken much longer than it should have. It had also eaten up most of his fuel. He was pretty sure he'd have enough to get back to Camp Seven, but after that . . .

He tapped on the fuel gauge and groaned when the needle didn't move. With Logan and the six-man crew packed into the plane, he'd be lucky to get airborne again. Trouble was, his Old Beauty was their only chance for rescue. All three fires were now raging out of control, spreading men and equipment dangerously thin. Every one of the big CL-215 water bombers had been sent south to battle the largest of the blazes—without them, fire would wipe out a string of small towns.

It was all about numbers now, and the Fire Boss had made his decision. The tiny First Nations settlement Andy and his men had been fighting so hard to protect had already been evacuated. Camp Seven and the thousands of acres of timber around it would be left to burn, and there was no one left but Mitch to rescue Logan and the crew.

Logan. He'd been telling himself she was safe with Andy, that he'd done the right thing when he left her behind, that she was better off on the ground than flying into the fire at his side. But what if . . .

No. He struggled to block the dark thoughts that crowded his mind. Thoughts of what Logan might be thinking and feeling while she waited, reliving her nightmares, trapped and helpless in the path of the fire. Instead, he told himself she was safe. Andy would see to that—if he could . . .

She had to be all right. Since the moment he'd left her, Mitch hadn't been able to stop thinking about Logan—the ready laughter in her eyes, the scent of her hair, the taste of her lips. *She had to be all right.*

"Just hang on, Lily. I'm coming." *I'm coming!*

* * *

The firestorm moved like a wild animal—a hungry beast. It leaped from tree to tree growing larger, faster, hotter. At Camp Seven, the manmade strip of rock and bare earth below the ridge slowed it, stopped it, tried to hold it. But the fire would not be held. It roared like a thousand angry tigers. Breathing smoke and flames, it sprang high into the trees. It snaked along the ground. It flew. *It won.*

Two days of hard work had bought Andy's crew an extra ten minutes. They huddled close together now, their backs to the lake, waiting. Everyone knew the icy cold water meant death, just as surely as the fire. Logan heard one of the men whisper a prayer, and another mutter, "We're done for."

"Knock it off," yelled Andy. "Walker's on his way. He'll get us out."

Logan wrapped her arms around her waist and stared up at the sky. Nothing but smoke. No yellow wings. No rumble of engine. Just the terrible roar of the fire. It swept over the ridge as she watched, a wall of flame fifty feet high.

Trees snapped and blazed. They crashed, burning, onto the canvas supply tent, igniting the cache of gasoline. The drums of fuel blew up with a force that shook the ground, sending firebrands and burning embers raining down on the water's edge.

This must be what war is like, thought Logan, backing slowly into the lake as the fire roared again. *Where are you, Mitch? You said you'd come back. You said I'd be safe here.* She wanted to scream. She longed to run. But there was no place to go. Just fire and water. Logan splashed into the lake and began to swim.

"Stay here," bellowed Andy, pointing up into the sky. "Look!"

She stood, waist-deep in the icy water, while Andy fished her hardhat off the lake bed and jammed it back onto her head. "Look!" he said again.

Smoke swirled, parted like a curtain, and then she saw it. A big, yellow goose of an airplane settling onto the water. *Mitch.*

The Beaver lurched to a stop twenty yards from where they stood. Half-running, half-swimming the little group reached the plane just as Mitch threw open the cargo door. Logan felt Andy's big arms around her waist, lifting, pushing her through the door. Mitch caught her, held her close for one long heart-beat, then dropped her into the passenger seat and dove for the controls. Too dazed to speak, she pulled the seat belt over her shoulder, fumbling with water-numbed fingers to fasten the buckle.

"Go!" hollered Andy, as he and the other men scrambled aboard, slamming the door behind them.

Mitch was already on the move. Logan watched as he hauled back on the stick, giving it everything he could until the old engine whined and groaned. When the pontoons finally eased off the water, the plane bounced like a skipping stone, then sank again. Swearing, Mitch taxied back across the lake, into the hungry jaws of the fire.

"We need to move some weight around," he yelled. "Andy, go starboard, will ya? I'm gonna try to rock that port float off the water."

Uncharacteristically quiet, Andy followed instructions.

As the plane lurched across the water again, engine scream-ing, Logan squeezed her eyes shut and whispered a prayer in one word: *"Fly!"*

A loud cheer went up behind her as they rose slowly into the air. Andy and his crew were laughing, slapping each other on the back, hooting at Mitch . . . but he didn't seem to hear the happy shouts that filled the plane. He didn't look up, didn't even move. Logan watched him for a moment and felt her own smile fade. He was hunched over the controls, his mouth set in a grim line.

She looked out the window. The air around them was gray with smoke, but she could see trees below. Green trees. No fire.

"Mitch? What's wrong?"

The engine answered for him, giving a loud, hungry burp. The plane shuddered in response, instantly silencing Andy and his men.

"We're running a bit low on gas." Mitch's voice stayed calm and steady as he tapped the fuel gauge. "I think we're going to land. *Now.*"

The engine burped again.

Forgetting all about the fires, Logan tried to remember everything Walt had taught her about emergency landings. *"That's the beauty of floats. All's you ever need is a patch o' water and a steady hand."* Clutching the armrests, she scanned the earth below, desperate for a glimpse of blue among the green.

"There!" said Mitch, as a long finger of water appeared on the horizon. He flipped a switch on the radio, spoke into his headset and listened for a moment, then gave their position as he brought the plane in low over the treetops. They were still a few yards from the water's edge when the engine gave a last, low *buzz.*

Suddenly, their world was eerily quiet. No one spoke. It felt to Logan as if they were somehow suspended, caught at the end of a heavenly string as the lake rushed up to meet them. Then came a splash, a surge of water against floats, and the Beaver rocked to a stop.

Behind her, the fire crew cheered again, thumping each other on the back, hollering good-natured insults at Mitch, until Andy threw open the cargo door. The sudden rush of fresh, piney air silenced their voices. Had anything ever smelled so good? Logan eagerly filled her lungs with the cool air, and promptly began to cough. It would likely be days before she'd be rid of the taste, the smell, the *feel* of the fire.

"You okay?" Mitch leaned toward her, resting his hand on her arm.

"Yeah, just glad to be alive . . . thanks to you. Now what?"

"Now we wait," answered Mitch. "It'll be morning before they can send a plane with more fuel. Better get ashore."

The crew from Camp Seven was already in the water, sloshing toward the rocks, but Logan was in no hurry to keep them company. With two layers of soggy clothing to make her skin clammy and her teeth chatter, the very thought of stepping into another frigid lake had her shivering uncontrollably.

"Don't worry." Mitch winked as he leaned close, pulling her into his arms. "I'll build a nice hot fire to keep you warm."

Chapter Sixteen

A fire was the last thing Logan wanted. Despite her goose bumps and chattering teeth, she was quite certain she'd be happy if she never had to see another blaze. But as night fell and the air grew cool, she found herself creeping closer to the flames. The heat felt good, warming her aching body and making her damp clothes steam. Soon, the coveralls she'd draped over a stake beside the fire would be dry and toasty warm—a welcome change from her shiver-inducing wet T-shirt and jeans.

When Mitch sat behind her, sheltering her in his arms, she didn't object, leaning back against him as her eyes fell shut, letting his warmth surround her.

"You okay?" he murmured.

"I am now . . . thanks to you."

"You sure? You sound a little shaky."

She shook her head and snuggled closer. More than his warmth, she longed for reassurance . . . for answers. She was shaky, all right. What would he do if he knew the real reason why?

Why not tell him? Give him a chance to explain? "Mitch, it—it's just . . ."

"Just what?"

His lips brushed her ear as he spoke, full of warmth and tenderness. How could such a brief touch hold so much promise, cause so much confusion? Senses reeling, she groped for an answer, something to buy her a little more time.

"I guess . . . it's Ryan. I'm sure they'll let him know where we are, that we're okay, but . . . I just wish we knew for sure that *he's* all right."

"He's fine." Mitch chuckled. "Better than fine, I'd say."

"Better? What do you mean?"

"I've got a feeling he's enjoying Red Lake. Bales' sister has a couple of teenagers of her own, y'know. Twins. Blond. *Female . . .*"

Logan nudged him with her elbow. "I get the picture."

"Yeah. So I figure he's having the time of his life. Once this is all over, we're probably going to have to *drag* the kid away from Red Lake."

Once this is all over. She had only to look up at the night sky to know it was far from over. Mitch had managed to get them out of the fire zone but not by much, and now an eerie, orange glow illuminated the smoke-shrouded horizon to the south and west of their tiny green haven. *Fire.* They'd be fools to let themselves think they were safe from its fury.

She stayed silent for a while, listening to the calming sounds of the night . . . a Great Horned owl, whoo-whooing in the forest, water lapping against the rocky shore. She watched flames dancing across the pine logs in their hastily constructed fire pit—a fearful beauty, warm and bright, masquerading as a friend while Andy and his crew snored peacefully just a few feet away.

"Talk to me, Lily. You've been through enough today. Let me help."

Lily again. She wasn't so sure she liked it anymore. Suddenly, she wasn't sure of anything, especially her own feelings. How could she justify doubting him while she sat wrapped in his arms, feeling warm and safe and . . . loved?

Slipping her hand into the pocket of her jeans, Logan touched the wadded-up claim form and knew she'd made her decision.

Mitch had a right to know what she'd discovered, and she had a right to know the truth. Not later, not someday, but now.

Her fingers curled around the sodden paper, pulling it free, smoothing it carefully against her knee . . . but not carefully enough. It fell apart in her hand.

"What's that?"

"I was hoping you'd tell me."

She felt the warmth of his chest, pressing intimately against her back, as he leaned forward to peer over her shoulder. The page, dimly illuminated by the light of the flickering fire, was barely readable.

"Looks as if it's seen better days. Want to give me a hint?"

"D'Or-On."

She held her breath, waiting. For what, she wasn't sure—some sort of surprised reaction, a sudden tension, an angry word. Instead, he held her a little closer, resting his chin on the top of her head.

"What're they up to now?"

"It . . . it's not so much what *they're* up to, as—"

He brushed the hair away from her face, traced the line of her jaw with his thumb. If she turned toward him, even a little, she knew his lips would find hers and then . . .

"As what?"

She drew a deep, ragged breath, resisting the urge to toss the scraps of paper into the fire. "As what they think *you're* up to."

He straightened, letting a rush of night air chill the space between them. Logan shivered.

"Me? What am I up to?"

She turned slowly to face him, certain now of only one thing—she'd know the truth if she could see it in his eyes. "The Walker Place. That's what they're calling Casey Lodge. Did you know that?"

Mitch recoiled as if she'd slapped him. "What? Who? I don't understand."

"I met a man today, Kip somebody. He works for D'Or-On, a geologist, I think he said. Mitch, I only wanted to see what they're up to, find out how close they're coming to lodge property. But then he called it the Walker Place, and he showed me copies of the claim forms. And you . . . you said you were doing it for us, for Gramps, but it's all in your name—*all* of it. And, and people think—"

"People?"

The sharply spoken word stung, but Mitch said nothing more, simply stared at her for a painfully long moment, his face a shadowy puzzle, his eyes fiercely bright with reflected firelight. At last, he pushed to his feet and stalked away from her, stopping just long enough to growl, "What do *you* think, Logan? That's what really matters, isn't it?"

"What's goin' on?" A few feet away, Andy rolled onto his back, grumbling sleepily. "S'matter?"

"Nothing. Everything's fine. Go back to sleep, okay?"

Stiff and aching, Logan struggled to her feet and followed Mitch into the night. By the time she caught up to him at the lakeshore, she was shivering violently.

"Go back to the fire, Logan."

"No. N-not without you. We need to s-settle this, Mitch. *Now.* I want to b-believe in you, in *us*. Don't make me the b-bad guy because I asked a q-question."

Mitch grabbed her hand, uttering an impatient grunt as he pulled her back up the beach and into the circle of warmth cast by the fire. "Take these," he said, grabbing the nearly dry coveralls and thrusting them into her hands, "and put them on. Then we'll talk."

Grateful, Logan stepped into the darkness once more, quickly shedding her T-shirt and jeans to don the comfortably warm clothing. The sturdy yellow fabric felt heavenly against her chilled skin.

Mitch was staring into the fire when she returned. He spoke

quietly as she settled herself on the ground beside him. "Do you mean it?"

She looked up at him, questioning.

"You said you want to believe in me, Logan. Do you mean it?"

She moved closer, resting her hand on his arm and meeting his gaze. This time, she saw much more than shadows and firelight in his eyes. She saw a little boy facing the world alone . . . a grown man afraid to trust his heart to another. "I said more than that, Mitch. I said I want to believe in *us*. Yes, I mean it. You'd know that if you just stopped to think."

She watched him struggle, knew from experience how difficult it was for him to share his thoughts with her. She'd seen it time and again with her kids at school, kids like Ryan . . . like Mitch must have been. *Trust me, Mitch. I won't let you down.*

She had to bite her lip to keep silent. Whatever happened next, it had to come from him. Logan knew she'd won the battle when his hand found hers and held tight.

"When we get home, I want you to look in Casey's desk."

Home. "Okay. What am I supposed to look for?"

"A white envelope. It's got some papers inside making your grandfather a full partner in *AirWalker.*"

"Oh, Mitch, I—"

"Don't! Just let me finish, okay?"

She nodded, reaching up to touch his cheek with her fingertips, overwhelmed by what she was hearing.

"Yes, the claims are staked in my name, but there was no other choice. Fees had to be paid and forms signed. Casey wouldn't listen, he—"

Mitch drew a deep breath, letting it out on a weary sigh. "Well, that's Casey. You know how he is. Going behind that old man's back was the hardest thing I ever did . . . he trusted me, y'know? But I couldn't stand by and watch him lose everything he's worked so hard for . . . everything *we've* worked so hard for. So I got a lawyer to draw up the papers giving him half-interest in *Air Walker*, and I put them in the back of his desk drawer. Gave a copy to Ruby, too, just in case. I think she thinks it's my will or something. Anyway, they're dated long before you—''

''Shh.'' Logan pressed her fingers against his lips. He didn't need to say more to convince her. Once upon a time, she'd been certain there was nothing in the world that meant more to Mitch than his Old Beauty. Now she knew better. His eyes widened as she rose to her knees and slipped her arms around his neck. ''Gramps always told me to trust my heart.''

She smiled, leaning close to drop a tender kiss on his lips. ''I sure do like it when he's right.''

''Good morning, city girl.''

Logan opened her eyes as the first long rays of sunshine broke through the clouds. She smiled sleepily, unsure, at first, of where she was or what had happened. It all came back in a frightening rush. *''The fire!''*

''Hey, take it easy.'' Mitch soothed her, stroking her hair and rocking gently. ''We're safe. It's all over. That rain put the fires out.''

''Rain?''

He laughed. ''You were sound asleep. Andy and the boys made a shelter of pine boughs to keep us dry. Couldn't save the campfire, though. You warm enough?

''Yeah, but . . . Ouch!'' Logan tried to move and groaned again. Bruised and stiff after yesterday's challenges, her body didn't seem to want to go anywhere. ''Uhnh . . . What truck hit me?''

''Stay put,'' said Mitch. ''There's nowhere to go. And anyway, I like the way you feel in my arms.''

''Mmm, I like it, too.'' Gingerly lifting one stiff arm, she reached up to touch his face. ''You need a shave.''

"And *you* need a kiss."

"All right, you two," bellowed Andy from somewhere close by. "Cut out the mushy stuff. Did ya forget you've got company? Speaking of which . . . Anybody hear a plane?"

"Uhnh," said Logan again, beginning to feel like a turtle, stuck on her back. "I do. Give me a hand up, will you?"

She didn't have to ask twice. Andy and three of his crewmen appeared, hauling her to her feet just in time to watch a red-and-white Otter make a graceful landing on the lake.

"Thanks, guys," said Mitch dryly. "Remind me I owe you for that."

Andy grinned, offering Mitch a hand up, too. "Something tells me you two'll have plenty of time for huggin' and kissin'. Right now, though, there's something a lot more important you need to do."

"He's right, Mitch."

"Oh, yeah?" Mitch looked down at her and frowned. "What's that?"

"Be my hero one more time—take us home for breakfast."

Epilogue

"Aw, zoiks, gimme a break! Don't you two ever quit?"

Ryan stomped into the boathouse, dumping an armload of life jackets into the lead boat before he turned to scowl at them again. "If it ain't bad enough—"

"Isn't," said Logan, letting her arms slide away from Mitch's neck. "If it *isn't* bad enough."

Ryan wrinkled his nose, pointedly ignoring the reminder. "If it *ain't* bad enough to find Casey kissin' Ruby in the kitchen, now I gotta watch you two go at it, too? Yuck-oh."

"Hey! Newlyweds are supposed to kiss a lot," said Mitch.

Ryan responded with a rude noise, beating a hasty retreat into the sunshine.

Logan couldn't help smiling. His smark-alecky demeanor hadn't changed one bit in the six weeks he'd been with them, but in every other way he was a much different person— stronger, more self-confident. Hard work and fresh air, combined with Ruby's good home cooking, had transformed a skinny, pale-faced child into a tanned and muscular young man.

When Gramps and Ruby surprised them with news of their engagement, Ryan had worked harder than anyone getting the new cabin finished and ready for the honeymoon. He'd even joined Gramps in some good-natured teasing that she and Mitch should stop stalling and "get the knot tied" too. All things considered, the kid had no one to blame but himself when he'd been called to duty as best man at the first double wedding in the history of Indigo Bay.

"I don't know, Mitch, seems to me Ryan was the one who said we should get married in the first place. Now all he does is complain."

"Yeah, well, I figure he's just jealous. Tough. Let him get his own girl."

"He still thinks we wrecked his chances in the girl-getting department by showing up in Red Lake when we did."

"Not wrecked," called Ryan from beyond the door, "just delayed. They kinda liked me in my suit the day of the wedding. You *did* say we'd be going back this weekend . . . right?"

"Yeah, kid, that's the plan. You might want to reconsider tagging along, though."

Reconsider? Logan frowned. "Wha—"

Mitch silenced her with a slow wink, just as Ryan turned to face them. "Oh, no, you don't! You promised. I ain't—"

"Logan talked me into letting her fly."

Ryan didn't miss a beat. "No!" Clasping both hands over his heart, he staggered backwards toward the water's edge. "I'm too young to die!"

Logan pulled her Jays cap off and whipped it at him. "Don't press your luck, kiddo. I might be forced to practice my aileron rolls while we're up there."

Mitch gasped. "No! *I'm* too young to die!"

"You got that right," said Logan, sliding her arms around his waist. "You promised me a lifetime, Mister, and I aim to collect."

Author's Note

It's a little-known fact that property ownership in Ontario's northland does not automatically include subsurface rights. Here, as in other remote areas of the world, prospectors may stake claims and mine ore deposits by tunneling beneath the surface owner's property. On the Canadian Shield, a land rich in gold, silver, nickel, even diamonds, the practice is perfectly legal.

You can learn more about mining in Ontario by visiting the Ministry of Northern Development and Mines web site at *www.on.gov.ca/MNDM*, or investigate the awesome world of forest fires and the men and women who fight them at the Canadian Wildfire Network, on line at *www.denendeh.com/ flycolor/wildfire*.

I would love to hear from you. Please write to me c/o Avalon Books, or send e-mail to *writerly@hotmail.com*.

—CHERYL COOKE HARRINGTON